Other Books by Ursula Hegi

The Vision of Emma Blau
Tearing the Silence
Salt Dancers
Stones from the River
Floating in My Mother's Palm
Unearned Pleasures and Other Stories
Intrusions

Hotel of the Saints

Stories

URSULA HEGI

Simon & Schuster
New York   London   Toronto   Sydney   Singapore

SIMON & SCHUSTER
Rockefeller Center
1230 Avenue of the Americas
New York, NY 10020

For information about special discounts for bulk purchases,
please contact Simon & Schuster Special Sales:
1-800-456-6798 or business@simonandschuster.com

Designed by Deirdre C. Amthor

Manufactured in the United States of America

1   3   5   7   9   10   8   6   4   2

Library of Congress Cataloging-in-Publication Data
Hegi, Ursula
Hotel of the saints : stories / Ursula Hegi.
p. cm.
Contents: Hotel of the saints—The end of all sadness—A woman's perfume—Stolen
chocolates—Doves—Freitod—Moonwalkers—A town like ours—
The juggler—For their own survival—Lower crossing
I. Title.

PR9110.9.H43 H68 2001
823'.914—dc21   2001042944

ISBN 0-684-84310-2

Some of the stories in this collection appeared in the following periodicals: "Hotel of the
Saints," Story; "The End of All Sadness," Triquarterly; "A Woman's Perfume," originally pub-
lished as "Collaborators," Louisville Review; "Doves," Prairie Schooner; "Freitod," Ms.; "A
Town Like Ours," Prairie Schooner; "The Juggler," Story; "For Their Own Survival," Louisville
Review. "Stolen Chocolates" was a selection of The Syndicated Fiction Project.

Acknowledgments

As always, I have valued the insights and comments I've received while working on these stories. A special thank you to my agents, Gail Hochman and Marianne Merola; to my editor, Mark Gompertz; to Olivia Caulliez, Deb Harper, Sue Mullen, and David Weekes; and to my husband, Gordon Gagliano.

For my son Adam

Contents

Hotel of the Saints

Hotel of the Saints

Lenny's mother, the starch queen, is baking for her brother's funeral: cinnamon cookies and blackberry pies, garlic bread and her own recipe of poppyseed strudel. Lenny loves watching his mother's freckled fists pummel the dough. Next to her, he feels anemic in his seminary clothes.

Across the kitchen, her two sisters are also baking to see their one brother, Leonard, off according to parish tradition—the bake-off of the starch sisters.

Early on, Lenny learned to dodge his Uncle Leonard, who was far too fussy and pious for him, who took it upon himself to fill the father role in Lenny's life, who gave him his name at birth, holy cards from his hotel gift shop on Easter Sundays, and a pocket watch when Lenny entered the Jesuit seminary four years ago.

"In a family of women," Uncle Leonard liked to say, "it's important for a boy to look up to a man."

But by the time Lenny was eleven, he was already half a head taller than his uncle and felt far more comfortable with the women in the family. The starch queen—after an impulsive marriage in her late thirties—had divorced Lenny's father, Otis,

17

two months before Lenny was born, eager to return to her sisters, who'd never married, and continue the pattern of their childhood. The Taluccio sisters always were close: when they were girls, they insisted on sharing the turret room on the third floor of their old Victorian by the Willamette River in Portland. Now each sister has a cluster of rooms she calls her own, but they convene in the tiled kitchen and on the wide porch that envelops three sides of the house.

Slender, strong women with firm arms, the Taluccio sisters laugh too loudly and slap men's backs when they greet them. They seldom speak of Otis, who moved away from Portland after the divorce and has never contacted the starch queen or his child. When Lenny was a boy, they sometimes saw the yearning for his father in his eyes, and they answered whatever questions he had about Otis—how Otis hated the rain; how Otis liked raspberries mixed in with sliced bananas; how Otis had a cat named Muffy when he was a boy; how Otis liked to drive with the windows open—and they helped Lenny imagine Otis in some dry, warm climate, working in a marina, or a car dealership. Amongst themselves, though, the starch sisters are sure Otis just continued to drift from one unemployment line to another, braking for spells of work just long enough to qualify him, once again, for unemployment checks.

Now that they're retired from their jobs at the post office and fabric shop and hardware store, the starch sisters like to play cards late into the night—just the three of them—sitting around the kitchen table with a bowl of pretzels and a bottle of Chianti. They pray with the same passion that they bring to their food and their card games, and they take pride in still belonging to the parish where they were christened, a parish so poor that the altar society has only one change of clothing for the Infant of Prague statue.

With their sister-in-law, Jocelyn, the starch sisters are patient, although she horrifies them with her helplessness. Forty years earlier, on her honeymoon, Lenny's Aunt Jocelyn gave up on getting her driver's license because she backed Uncle Leonard's car into a tree while he was teaching her how to parallel-park. It has been like that with everything—Aunt Jocelyn folds whenever she gets agitated. To keep herself from getting agitated, she must take pills that Uncle Leonard used to mark off on an index card taped to the refrigerator. He used to do everything for her—drive her to mass every morning, schedule doctors' appointments, bring her to the grocery store, buy clothes for her, choose books from the library so she'd be content while he ran the hotel and gift shop.

Back when the starch queen was pregnant with Lenny, Aunt Jocelyn talked about wanting a baby too, but Uncle Leonard reminded her, "Not in your condition." To appease her, he planted a rose garden on the semicircle of lawn in front of his hotel, prize-winning varieties of hybrid tea roses that he ordered from a catalogue—selecting them not for their colors but because their names attracted him: Command Performance, Sterling Silver, King's Ransom, Golden Gate, Apollo, Century Two, Royal Highness, Texas Centennial.

But Aunt Jocelyn never even watered the roses. He was the one who would fertilize them in March and September; spray against rust and mildew, aphids and spider mites; cut off their weak branches in the fall and prune the strong canes by a third; cover them with pine needles for the winter.

❧ ❧ ❧

His uncle's death has given Lenny an acceptable excuse to leave the seminary for a while to help Aunt Jocelyn get the hotel ready for sale. Lenny has some doubts about being in the seminary; for some time now he has felt that, if only he could get a few months away from there, he might figure things out. What he thought he wanted was much clearer to him before he entered the order, and in the four years since, he's been trying to get back to it—that undefinable sense of one source.

Faith has become complicated: it has moved from his heart into his head, where it abides, fed by scriptures and prayers. But his heart keeps forgetting, and he no longer feels the certainty of faith that belonged to him as a boy.

Lenny has confided this to only two people—carefully to his adviser, Father Richard Bailey, and far more openly to his best friend, Fred Fate. Fred is two days older than Lenny and entered the seminary—so he'll tell you—"because then everyone will have to call me Father Fate." But you can see Fred's faith in his walk, hear it in his laughter. In comparison, Lenny's faith is puny. He feels constricted by his black clothes, yearns for canary yellow and a shade of orange so intense it's vulgar, for lush green and the kind of blue you can climb into.

The morning of Leonard's funeral, Fred checks out a monkmobile—his name for any one of the long, well-maintained cars in the Jesuit garage—and meets Lenny at the starch queen's house for breakfast. Aunt Jocelyn already sits at the table, hands folded on her chiffon skirt. Her cousin, Bill, has brought her. Lenny is not used to seeing his aunt in black. Most of her clothes are white, and with her pallid complexion—"indoor skin," the starch sisters call it—she usually looks like the overexposed photo of a lady missionary. But the black fabric makes her skin look even more faded. As Lenny reaches for his aunt's hands and kisses her on both cheeks, he wishes he could sketch her: she has the kind of face that comes at you in eyes, all eyes.

The starch queen's best friend from high school, Cheryl Albott, arrives with two tablecloths and stacks of matching cloth napkins that still have the manufacturer's stickers on them. Cheryl, who works in the customer-service department at Sears, has a front row opera subscription together with the starch queen. For decades, the two have attended every opening night in Portland, and for decades Cheryl has given the starch queen refunds for fancy outfits that she buys to wear at the opera or other special occasions and brings back a day or two later.

Ever since Lenny became a Jesuit, Cheryl has looked at him with reverence and called him "Father," though Lenny has explained to her that he's a brother, and that brothers—though they take vows of poverty, chastity, and obedience just like Fathers—do not administer the sacraments or give absolution.

Cheryl's arrival makes Lenny notice his mother's dark tailored suit with the lace collar. "New?" he inquires, though he doesn't really want to know.

The starch queen fondles her lapel, winks at Cheryl. "Only the best for Leonard's funeral."

At the grave site, Lenny holds Aunt Jocelyn's elbow. She is younger than the starch queen, yet she can barely walk alone and stumbles frequently. Her cousin tells Lenny that Aunt Jocelyn can't prepare meals for herself, that she refuses to move out of the hotel although her side of the family has found a safe place for her to live.

"It's run by the nuns. Your aunt could go to mass every day. You know how important mass is to her."

"We don't have to rush her."

"She's not fit to live alone. She doesn't even use the phone."

"I'll look after her while I work on the hotel."

"And how long will that be?"

After the funeral, when the starch queen tries to pile seconds on Fred's plate, he diverts her by asking, "Did you know that Lenny hardly eats at the seminary? Don't you think he's getting awfully thin?"

The serving spoon with manicotti still in motion, the starch queen changes its course from Fred to Lenny, who mouths a silent *fuck-you-very-much* across the table to his friend.

" . . . working too hard," Fred goes on. "Always running around. Looking peaked. Don't you think so?"

Cheryl from the refund department gets that *bless-me-Father* look in her eyes, and the manicotti on Lenny's plate is joined by a chunk of oily garlic bread.

But Lenny gets even when Fred is ready to leave. "Father Fate is crazy about your cooking," he tells the starch sisters. "You should hear him. He's always raving about you."

Promptly, the starch sisters gather by the counter to wrap leftover lasagna, eggplant parmigiana, and poppyseed strudel for Father Fate, stacking everything in a shopping bag for him to take back with him.

"I can't possibly eat all this," Fred groans.

But Lenny urges the starch sisters on. "Father Fate is always so modest."

Hotel of the Saints

"You'll get hungry tonight," the starch queen promises Fred.
"You can share it with the other Fathers," Cheryl says.

Wrought-iron balconies, too narrow for anyone to stand on,
decorate the façade of Uncle Leonard's hotel on N.E. Sandy
Boulevard. Roses, the size of grapefruits, cover the slope in
front, and the gift shop is crammed full of religious pictures and
enough statues to outfit four cathedrals. It's only a few blocks
from the Grotto—Sanctuary of Our Sorrowful Mother—where
visitors like to ride the huge elevator up a sheer cliff and walk
the scenic pathway lined with the Mysteries of the Rosary.

During the year of Uncle Leonard's chemotherapy, the
hotel has grown shabby despite the efforts of Mr. Wolbergsen,
the handyman, who moved to his sister's in Walla Walla when
Uncle Leonard closed the hotel three months before his death.

After Aunt Jocelyn goes to sleep, Lenny wanders through
the rooms—all identical, with pale-gray walls, faded curtains,
and a single painting above the dresser, usually of either Mary
or Jesus with a liver-colored heart weeping through a gap in the
tunic. Lenny settles himself in the room closest to his aunt's
apartment in case she needs help during the night, but when he
wakes up, it's already eight and she's in the kitchen, dressed for
mass, stirring a concoction of lard and sunflower seeds on the
gas stove.

He feels queasy. "I'll eat later," he says.

When he drives her to church in Uncle Leonard's old station wagon, she sits stiffly next to him, handbag clutched to her
chest, eyes vacant. During mass, she keeps frowning and rub-

23

bing one finger up and down the ridges as if to erase them. On the way home, Lenny stops with her at the hardware store and buys ten gallons of pale-gray interior latex while she lingers above the paint charts, pointing to bright pinks and reds. She won't leave until he buys a quart of fuchsia.

At the hotel, she scoops the cooled lard and seeds into a pie tin and sets it out on the windowsill.

"Oh, it's for the birds," Lenny says.

She shields her eyes. Peers at him.

After he fries eggs and butters her toast, he begins with the renovation, starting in the last room down the hall. Soon, his eyes ache from the relentless gray, and his arms feel heavy when he raises the brush. He wishes he could accept everything about the Jesuits. Or nothing. While Fred chooses what he believes, Lenny feels uneasy in the middle. Yet, whenever he pictures himself leaving the order, he gets sweaty and afraid that his faith is not strong enough to stand on its own, that he needs the frame of the church as much as his uncle needed the props of religious statues and holy cards.

There is something about hard work and bone-aching tiredness that appeals to him, because, gradually, it blots his doubts. Specks of gray settle in his nostrils, his eyebrows, in the fine hairs on his arms. He swears he's breathing paint.

Late afternoon, when he showers, he uses up four tiny cakes of hotel soap. Ready to cook dinner for his aunt and himself, he hobbles into the kitchen and finds Aunt Jocelyn sitting at the table, a can of tuna in front of her. He gets the opener, mixes the fish with mayonnaise, onion curls, and celery seeds. In the cupboard he finds a jar of pimentos and dices them, sprinkling them across the tuna salad.

"That's how the starch queen likes to make it," he tells Aunt

Jocelyn. "I miss cooking. In the seminary, everything is served to us."

After dinner, Aunt Jocelyn rests in a long canvas chair on the flagstone terrace. She closes her eyes while Lenny waters the rose garden. The leaves look even greener when they are wet. He would love to see that color against the somber walls he painted today—not just green, but other colors, so lush you wouldn't want to wash them from your skin after painting an entire room with them.

Fred is nearly two hours late when he stops by the following afternoon in yet another monkmobile, a Chrysler this time. It has been his turn to drive the nuns from the convent school to the blood drive.

"You look . . . drained," Lenny says.

Fred laughs. "The nuns have been asking about you." He sits down on the floor and watches Lenny paint another wall. "Let's see. . . ." He counts on his fingers. "There's Sister Mary of the Most Blessed Heart Exposed, Sister Margaret of the Holy Shroud Exposed, Sister Catherine of the Immaculate Blood—"

"Exposed," Lenny says, knowing how Fred likes to mangle the nuns' names and include "exposed," even when he takes phone messages at the seminary. "Now—who really asked after me?" Lenny wants to know.

"Just Father Bailey and that old feisty sister who always demands two cups of orange juice after relinquishing her blood."

"Sister Barbara."

"Of the Most Sacred Thorns—"

"Exposed."

✤ ✤ ✤

His third day of painting, Lenny mixes a few drops of Aunt Jocelyn's fuchsia paint with the gray, but they're not enough to soak
up the starkness. When his aunt comes to watch him, she dips
one finger into the fuchsia can and holds it close to the window.
They look at each other; she tries to smile, but her lips tremble.
Reaching for Lenny's brush, she dips it into the fuchsia and
draws a brilliant smudge on the wall by the window.

Lenny reaches out to steady her, but she's not nearly as wob-
bly as usual, and he doesn't know what to do except join her.
When they finish early that evening, her white culottes and
matching blouse are splattered with fuchsia. The entire room is
fuchsia, including the trim. Without stopping to clean up, they
drive to the hardware store, buy cans of blue, yellow, red. In the
morning they go to mass, but Aunt Jocelyn is eager to get home
and mix the color for their next project—a rich sun-orange that
seems to cover the walls much faster than gray.

They sit down to eat lunch, streaks of brightness in her hair
and on her blouse. When Lenny cleans the counter, he finds
two pill bottles on top of the kitchen trash. Both are more than
half full. He takes them out.

"I feel better without them," she says.

"Have you talked to your doctor about this?"

"I found the warning slips from the pharmacy in Leonard's
desk . . . a list of everything that can go wrong." She gets up,
tears the index card her husband used to mark her pills, and
holds out her hand for the bottles. "Don't tell anyone."

"At least let me keep them till you've checked with your
doctor."

"It's my doctor who put me on them."

"How long since you've stopped?"

"The day we buried Leonard."

At first he considers calling the starch queen for advice, but with each day Aunt Jocelyn looks so much better—no longer so helpless but oddly energized—that he worries less. And by the time the starch sisters visit, carrying homemade fettuccine and a gallon of tomato sauce with many tiny meatballs, he can brag about how Aunt Jocelyn walks to the library now to choose her own books, how she calls cabs that take her to the supermarket.

"The first time I heard her on the phone," he says, "I was amazed."

"You're good for her," the starch queen says. "Everyone in the family knows that Jocelyn hasn't used the phone since she dialed a wrong number twelve years ago."

"More like thirteen years," one of the starch sisters says.

Lenny feels content working with Aunt Jocelyn on transforming the rooms. That's what he had thought being a Jesuit would be like—using his skills to help others, living a simple life. That's what drew him to enter the order. His faith used to thrive in an atmosphere of simplicity—doing things for one another as his mother and her sisters did within their community and parish all those years he was growing up—but in the seminary that simplicity has become lost to a life filled with comforts, to days filled with philosophy and theology classes. He knows he could stay in the order forever and have all his needs taken care of—from money for books, to monkmobiles at his disposal, to the rich meals that are anything but simple.

HOTEL OF THE SAINTS

✤ ✤ ✤

One night he dreams Aunt Jocelyn is standing by the refrigerator, staring at a blank index card. She raises both arms, howls as she pounds her fists against the refrigerator door. He catches her fists, pulls her toward him. Her fine hair falls away from her face, and he can see into her soul. "The hospital is on the roof," he tries to say, but he can't separate his lips. With one hand he holds his aunt's wrists to keep her from hurting herself; with the other he strokes her face.

When he wakes up, he decides to call her doctor, but as soon as he sees his aunt in the kitchen, his concerns vanish. She has this secret little smile, and when she tells him to come with her, he follows her toward the gift shop. She's wearing the shirt and culottes she has designated as painting clothes—streaked with every color she's used so far. With each project she has become more vibrant, more muscular.

"What is it?" he asks her.

She doesn't tell him until they're inside the shop, surrounded by his uncle's religious kitsch. Then the words tumble from her. "I have this idea, a wonderful idea, Lenny. . . . We'll decorate each room after a different saint."

"It'll be difficult to sell the hotel."

She shakes her head and says what Lenny has already begun to suspect. "I'm keeping the hotel."

"It's too much work for you alone."

She watches him, silently. Then she smiles as if she'd just figured something out and touches one finger to his heart. "It has to be authentic. . . ."

Lenny sees himself as an altar boy, feeling holy while kneeling in front of the Sacred Heart of Jesus statue, whose toes were smudged from all the kisses people had pressed on them, and whose heart was covered with fake rubies that sparkled when you lit one of the votive candles.

"The decor," she says, "we'll make the decor authentic—so that it doesn't offend believers. They need to feel . . . confirmed when they stay at the hotel."

"Maybe that's the challenge." He nods. "To make it so authentic that the kitsch amuses some and makes others think they've arrived in their own heaven."

Fred is enthusiastic about the idea—"a pious sacrilege," he calls it—and he's eager to help. The first room, St. Anthony, is easy enough to put together—a basket with things previous guests have lost: keys, glasses, pens, hats.

The tiny bar next to the lobby they christen Mary Magdalene, and from there it seems only logical that the breakfast room is called Last Supper. "Service for thirteen," Lenny declares, though there are only eleven chairs around the long table. When Fred haunts secondhand stores in downtown Portland, he returns with two wooden chairs.

The honeymoon suite is named after Maria Goretti, who died very young while defending her honor. There is a room for St. Simon Stock, the hermit who lived in a tree trunk. Next to the bed, Aunt Jocelyn has set up a lava lamp on top of the tree stump that Fred brought in a monkmobile.

They call the men's room in the lobby St. Peter. When they try to find an equally appropriate name for the women's room, they don't come up with anything suitable and finally settle on two unisex bathrooms—both St. Peter. The only room that is painted entirely in white is the laundry room, named Immaculate Conception.

Some of their other ideas are too outrageous to follow through, but they laugh discussing them. "Would you hang this up in a church?" is their test question for quality control. "That's irreverent," expresses their approval. And Aunt Jocelyn will invariably say, "You better believe it."

The starch sisters take Aunt Jocelyn to the fabric store, where she buys entire bolts of bright prints. At their Victorian, they help her cut and sew curtains for the hotel. The ones for St. Francis's room have a forest pattern. It's the most elaborate room in the hotel. Propped in front of a painting of St. Francis are stuffed birds and an insipid wooden seagull. A plastic flamingo with a ribbon around its neck hangs above the bed. Lenny paints the floor with splotches to simulate bird shit, and Fred mounts a bird feeder to the outside of the window.

In St. Agnes's room the curtains have a design of baby lambs to symbolize the virginal purity of the sad plaster saint, whose eyes are turned up so far that you see only the whites, and whose hands are folded in front of her chest so that her fingertips point up in the same direction as her nose.

Lenny's favorite room is St. Sebastian's. He paints arrows around the windows, and Aunt Jocelyn hangs a basket of arrows across the wall from the bed. In the bathroom they install arrows as hooks for robes and replace the plastic toilet seat with an old wooden one. It has a crack that will pinch you if you don't sit sideways.

Hotel of the Saints

Fred helps with the painting of St. Stephen's room, named after the very first martyr. "You see, what it is," Fred explains, drawing the brush across the wall, "is that those martyrs were basically lazy. They wanted the quick way to glory. . . ."

"None of that waiting around for decades of drudgery like the rest of us mortals," Lenny says.

"But think of the ones who didn't make it," Aunt Jocelyn says.

"You'll make it," Lenny blurts.

They both stare at him.

He blushes. She'll make it, he thinks, if I stay here with her; maybe then she'll get well. He is awed by her courage—or is it foolishness, blind foolishness?—to burst from a life that has sheltered her for so long.

Fred arches his eyebrows.

"I wasn't talking about martyrdom," Lenny says.

"Those hundreds of poor souls . . ." His aunt sighs. "Those who waited for their chance at martyrdom—"

"And found no takers." Fred laughs. "No Huns or Romans who'd relieve them of their heads or tear off their limbs."

His third week at the hotel, Lenny wakes at dawn to sounds outside. In the garden, Aunt Jocelyn is tearing out the rosebushes. She's wearing her painting clothes and leather work-gloves that are too big for her.

"What are you doing?"

"I'm not taking care of Leonard's roses."

"I can water them. I don't mind." He steps between her and the next bush.

"Lenny . . ." She shields her eyes, though the sun hasn't come out yet. Her bare arms are scratched from her wrists to her elbows. "I don't want to look at Leonard's roses." She proceeds to yank bushes from the earth. "I've called a landscaping service to fix it up."

Lenny tries to predict the starch sisters' reaction once they find out about all this.

The starch queen: "If that's what Jocelyn wants."

One starch sister: "Doesn't she look better all around?"

The other starch sister: "Some lasagna will be good for her."

Lenny seizes a bush as close to the roots as possible to keep from getting scratched, and as he pulls, hard, he feels he's dislodging something deep within himself. By the edge of the lawn, he helps Aunt Jocelyn pile the bushes into a mound, tall enough for a funeral pyre. Three men in Easter-green overalls arrive in a lettered truck to lay squares of Easter-green sod into the spaces where the roses used to grow.

"This is what it looked like when I moved in here," Aunt Jocelyn tells Lenny after the men have left. She steps out of her sandals. Lying down, she extends her arms above her head and rolls down the slope—a whirling canvas.

Lenny runs after her, afraid she'll tumble into the street, but she stops by herself where the lawn meets the sidewalk. The sun is on her face. Bits of grass stick to her clothes.

"You ought to try it, Lenny." She squints up at him. Smiles.

"Maybe some other time."

"Once you're old enough?"

"Right," he says and has to laugh.

"Feel this." She curls her long toes into the thick grass. "Just feel this, Lenny."

Hotel of the Saints

He unties his shoes, sits down, fingers splayed, palms sinking into the lawn. For an instant there, it feels as though the ground were tilting beneath him—a seesaw kind of tilting—and as he instinctively braces it with his body, Lenny knows this is the kind of tilting that may happen to you again, and all you have is your faith that each time your body will find some new balance.

The End of All Sadness

And when I saw him that first time sleeping on the ground by the pond there was light all around him and I stood watching him till he opened his eyes and poured me the light and then he strapped his clothes and blanket into his tarp and followed me to my apartment and the food he cooked for me nourished me more than anything I had eaten for years. Already the weight of the lonely flesh was falling from me as his beauty filled me and even at the mall my customers said I had a glow that lit up the whole Sears.

He was kind to my daughter and though she's ten he let her ride on his bare shoulders when we walked down the hill to swim in the pond and after one week we were a family and soon we had a canary and two hamsters that a woman gave us at the Laundromat and he found work in custodial at the mall and bought salmon for us and I borrowed three wedges of lemon from my cousin next door and he grilled the salmon on the balcony in the evening while my daughter painted her toenails purple and pink and when we rode in my car to get ice cream we looked like a family and it was the end of all sadness.

The End of All Sadness

Outside the kitchen window he fastened a hummingbird feeder and we watched the Jesus-birds hang from the sky like fire lanterns with their chests skin instead of feathers and their long beaks immersed in the sweet red and their wings whirring waiting as if someone had folded them around the core of a heart.

He wept when he left marks on my face because I'd smiled at the UPS man the way my mama had taught me about being polite and smiling when someone is nice to you and he told me he'd rather kill himself than ever hurt me again and that he ought to leave me except he loved me too much and I held his head between my palms and kissed his eyes and cried stay with me. All that night he held me and brushed my hair for me in the morning and brought me French toast in bed and after my daughter went to school he loved me as if I were expensive glass and I felt his light pour through me as I rose to the surface of my skin.

I slept and when I woke my daughter was lying on her bed shivering and wrapped in my raincoat though it was summer and I explained to her how he couldn't bear to watch me talk to other men and he came into her room and gave us money for white dresses and married me that Sunday by the pond. My cousin said she couldn't come but he said you have me now and the minister stood with his back to the water but we could see the green ripples were wind swished across the surface and the green glint of sun in broken bottle glass and I marveled that a man so beautiful had come to choose me. After being loved like that I knew I'd die if I ever had to return to the sadness and when my daughter wouldn't speak to him at the Denny's where he took us in our white dresses for our wedding lunch he reminded me that she would not always be with me but that he would.

HOTEL OF THE SAINTS

He was my husband then and he painted the front door and fixed the TV and disconnected the phone and hung a ceiling fan above our bed that spun its wings all night till the room pulsed like a Jesus-bird and I could see the reflection of the pulse in the windows and in his eyes and feel it low in my belly. He took us to the carnival and bought my daughter cotton candy and a monkey-on-a-stick and he kept my keys and drove me to work and picked me up with his beautiful jealous love that no one has ever loved me with and I felt strong and special as I walked beneath his gaze and when my cousin turned from his greeting though he looked respectable now I stopped visiting next door and he said there's a tree in Arizona where miracles are starting to happen and maybe we'll move there and start over without suspicious neighbors but he didn't know what kind of tree and what kind of miracles only that it was south of Tucson and that someone in jail had told him and he was sorry he hadn't thought to ask.

He cashed our paychecks and shopped for our food and cooked for the three of us my own family he said my very own while my daughter did her homework and when we ate he asked her to tell him about school but the happier I got the smaller my daughter looked and I said give her time when she wouldn't talk to him and he slapped her mouth and I said no but I understood that he was like those women in India who jumped off a burning train and were hit by an oncoming train. I read about them in the paper a long time ago but I think of them often and when I told him about them and I said that's just like you getting away from one misfortune only to fall right in the path of the next he said but it's different now because you've come along.

The End of All Sadness

I don't tell him that sometimes I'm grateful he had his hard-luck life that kept him away from the world even though it's un-just because it began when his fiancée cheated on him and he shook her wanting to hear the truth and then she was dead but it means he has come to me new and that I'm his only wife ever be-cause if he hadn't been in jail all these years another woman would have found him long before me and married him.

And even now when I see the rage climb into his eyes it's never for long and most of the time I know how to ease him out of it by taking his hands and bringing them around my breasts and motioning my daughter out of the living room as I pull him into me because then his rage spins into light and fills me and makes me powerful and even when I can't harness his rage and it crushes both of us I always remind myself that he'll only love me so much more the next day. What I've come to recognize is that moment when the power can shift and when he'll either move into me or shatter me with his rage and it's that moment that has become the most exciting thing in my life because if I can turn that rage into light I own him and each time I own him adds to the sum of holding him.

And whenever he talks of leaving because he is afraid of hurting me worse I smile and pull him toward me and some-times I forget my daughter is in the room because there's no air for anyone but me and him but then his hands are on me and I feel her shrinking away a silent shadow in my raincoat. Some nights she walks in her sleep and I find her on the sidewalk with her hamsters and I hold her and tilt her face to the night and show her how to watch for a shooting star so she can make her secret wish for a miracle of her own.

A Woman's Perfume

The summer after my parents' divorce, my father took me to the yellow hotel near Trieste where we used to stay every July with my mother. The balcony of our suite overlooked the Riviera di Barcola, and from my bedroom, I could see the Adriatic Sea and the cliff with the white *castello* where Maximilian of Hapsburg and Charlotte of Belgium had lived a hundred years ago.

The hotel was a favorite of other German tourists, and whenever my father and I sat in the dining room, we'd hear more German than Italian. Even here, people were gossiping about the Shah of Iran and his third wife, Farah Diba. German newspapers and magazines had been speculating ever since the wedding last December that the Shah would divorce the young architecture student—as he had his previous wives—unless she produced a son. Already Farah Diba was pregnant. But what if she gave birth to a daughter?

My leather dictionary was small enough to carry in my palm, and I would rehearse those vibrant Italian words when my father and I shopped in the open market. I loved the rapid voices rising above the bins of bright fruits and vegetables, the metal trays filled with fish, the stands with jewelry and combs and lace. Italy was far more exciting than my own country with its somber, guttural sounds that often were like the beginning of a cough. I liked the laugh of the dark-eyed men who sold us tiny golden-crisp fish that crackled when I ate them whole; the plum-shaped tomatoes that still hung on wilting vines; the taut peaches and grapes whose juice would run down my neck when I'd bite into them. Some vendors said I carried the sun in my hair and tried to tease me into bartering a touch of my blond hair in return for so many lire off whatever I wanted to buy. Though my father would shake his head, I'd usually laugh back at the men and let the quick warmth of brown fingers into my long hair.

Every morning, my father and I played a game of tennis behind the hotel and ate the breakfast he fixed for us on our balcony; then I'd run into the blue-green water of the Adriatic Sea, swim out far into the waves, and let them carry me back to shore. The day I got my period—my fourth one ever—I swam as usual, waving to my father, who was setting out for one of his solitary hikes along the beach, carrying his anger and grief in the stiff angle of his arms. He never talked about my mother, and if I mentioned her at all, he'd get very quiet. Sometimes I was afraid he'd just keep walking on that beach, past the city of Trieste, past the border, and into Yugoslavia.

About an hour after my swim, my insides began to cramp with pains that pulsed into my legs, my chest. I tried lying on my bed, sitting up, walking. Nothing helped. One hand against the wall, I made it to our balcony and scanned the long ribbon of sand for my father. But another cramp took hold, and I dropped to my knees. Crying, I curled up by the railing, knees pulled against the front of my swimsuit, wishing my mother were here. But she was far away, in India on a medical project. That's what my mother had dreamed of doing when, at age nineteen, she became a nun: travel to exotic regions to help the poor who really needed her. I'd grown up knowing that—had it not been for falling in love with my father, the convent accountant, and being surprised by motherhood—my mother would have left Germany long ago to work in those exotic regions with other nuns. Instead, she ended up assisting doctors who took out the tonsils and set the broken bones of ordinary Germans.

Sometimes I thought she had divorced me as much as my father, leaving both of us behind when she met a group of American Mormon missionaries in Berlin, who sent people like my mother to foreign countries where she could heal far more interesting ailments than any she might find in Germany.

But maybe this pain that felt as though my body were turning itself inside out would interest my mother. And maybe the lush setting would contribute to making me a worthwhile patient. Another cramp ran through me, and I moaned, certain I was about to die. *My mother, all dressed in black, stands by my open grave, sobbing as my coffin is lowered into the wormy earth. "I'm sorry, Christa. I'm so sorry. How can I go on living without my only child?" As she tries to throw herself across my coffin, three men—no, four—have to hold her back. . . .*

Hot gusts of wind blew in from the sea, carrying specks of sand and the smell of fish. My lips felt dry, *but my mother's cool hand elevates my head as she guides a glass of lemonade to my lips. "Here, drink this, Christa." Her thin face looks tired from traveling so far to be with me. But at least she is here. Worried that she has not arrived in time to prevent my terrible illness, she*

A Woman's Perfume

whispers, "You need help, don't you?" And I moan, louder, just for
her, just to keep her here. Here—

"You need help, don't you?" The voice, I could hear the
voice clearly—but it no longer belonged to my mother. And the
woman's hair, a lighter shade of blond than my mother's, was
not short but braided back into a chignon. She had red-red lips,
and she was studying me across the partition from the next bal
cony. "I'll be right there."

After her face vanished, I heard the scraping of a chair being
dragged onto the balcony. As she climbed across the wall, her
back to the sea that lay three floors beneath us, she talked herself through it: "Careful now, Anneliese . . . don't look down
there. You know how you are with heights. Easy, now." The
hem of her white dress flared above her high-heel sandals, and
the butterfly clasp of her belt glittered in the sun.

"There, now." She leapt down on our side of the balcony.
"There, now." Kneeling by my side, she put her arms around
me and helped me to sit up.

I could smell her perfume—not flowery like most perfumes, but like the kind of breath you want to hold in your
lungs for a long time.

She led me inside and settled me on the sofa, two pillows
beneath my feet. "Where does it hurt, *Liebchen?*"

I motioned to my belly, my chest, my legs. Another cramp
made me draw up my knees. "But it never hurts like this when I
have my period."

She touched the strap of my swimsuit. "You didn't go swimming, did you?" She sounded alarmed.

"For a while."

"But it's the worst thing you can do, going into salt water

41

when you have your period. It draws your blood right out of you. Some women try to bring on their bleeding by soaking their feet in salt water. Don't you know that?"

"No."

"Putting your whole body into salt water . . ." She clicked her tongue. "Poor girl. Didn't your mother tell you this?"

"She—she went to India. Before I started periods."

"Is she joining you and your father here?"

"She used to come here . . . but they're divorced now."

"Just when you need her most," she said softly.

Sudden tears crowded the inside of my head. I turned my face aside.

"Men don't know about things like that. At least not how to explain them to a young girl."

Her name was Frau Hilger, Anneliese Hilger, and she took hold of my life from that moment on. She brought me oval pills from her apartment, made peppermint tea, buttered crisp *Zwieback*, and made me rest on our living-room sofa with two of her German fashion magazines. When my father opened the door, she was frying paper-thin veal cutlets, *Wiener Schnitzel*, in our kitchen.

"Your daughter is doing better," I heard her whisper before he could say anything.

"What happened? Christa didn't drown or—"

"I have her lying down." Taking his hand into hers, she steered him toward the sofa where I was lounging, quite comfortable by now, surrounded by cups and plates and magazines.

"My God," my father said.

I sighed. Draped one hand across my forehead.

"What happened to you, *Kind?*"

Frau Hilger winked at me, then smiled at my father as if she

42

had separate secrets with each of us. "Women's problems."

He took off his glasses. Busied himself cleaning them with his handkerchief.

"Your daughter should have never gone into salt water. It pulls all the blood out of you at once."

"Do you need anything?" As he tucked my hair behind my ears, he looked as if he were about to ask me something else, but Frau Hilger laid one slender hand on his arm and drew him toward the kitchen.

"Let me pour you some Chianti," I heard her say. "Sit down. We'll eat soon."

"I couldn't impose."

But she shook her head, firmly. "It's at times like these that a girl needs the friendship of a woman."

That midday meal, it was just the three of us, but when we entered the dining room in the evening, she waved us over to the table where she was sitting with a man. My father hesitated. But then she waved again, and he patted his brown mustache to make sure it was in place as he started toward her. Frau Hilger's lipstick made her white teeth look even whiter, and she was wearing white again, this time a silk suit with a scarf and that elegant butterfly belt. To me, she seemed like the kind of woman who always wears belts, even with coats.

She invited us to sit and eat with her and her husband, a quiet man with thick eyelids and thick earlobes that gave his face a sleepy look. After greeting us politely, he said little while she recommended the *spezzatino di maiale*—a stew made with pork and olives—and asked my father about his work as an accountant for a boarding school.

Over dessert she told my father, "I admire a man who takes on the responsibility of being a parent." Looking straight at her husband, she said, "I've never been fortunate enough to—"

"Don't," he said.

Her lips trembled.

"Don't, Anneliese." He tapped his fingers against the starched tablecloth.

"I've never been fortunate enough to birth children." Her eyes shimmered with tears when she looked at me as if I were the kind of daughter she would have wanted for herself, the daughter she would have never left behind; but soon she was laughing again with her red-red lips.

While Herr Hilger was getting even more silent, my father was talking more than he did when we were alone, and his shoulders were no longer stiff. A few times her ringed hand slid along the back of my father's chair—not touching his neck, though her fingers flexed as if already rehearsing. When we stood up to leave, her husband picked up her purse from the table and handed it to her without grazing her skin.

In the lobby she pressed a few of her oval pills into my hand—"Just in case, *Liebchen*,"—and gave my father two tickets. "There's a cruise in Grignano Bay tomorrow afternoon. Herr Hilger and I would be so delighted if you joined us."

My father stared at the tickets as if weighing their value. Perhaps she already guessed that he was not a man who could let anything fall to waste. I'd seen him finish burned pancakes my mother wanted to throw out, follow her from room to room to switch off the lights she left on—sometimes on purpose to tease him.

Frau Hilger smiled and curved one arm around me. "The statue of San Giusto lies at the bottom of Grignano Bay. But there's no need to decide now. After all—this is a vacation. A time to be spontaneous. If you're not there, Herr Hilger and I'll amuse ourselves. But just in case, I'll bring a picnic for all of us."

All of us. From that day on, all our encounters felt choreographed by Frau Hilger. Mornings, she'd call a greeting to us across the wall between our balconies. She'd insist on cooking the midday meal for us—usually German recipes—in her suite, which was the same size as ours, with two bedrooms and a living room and kitchen. In the evenings, we'd eat *rigatoni* or *cannelloni* with fish or chicken in Trieste or in the dining room of our hotel. When we'd sun ourselves on the beach, it would be next to the Hilgers. While he'd read biographies of composers and I'd swim in the sea, Frau Hilger and my father would stroll along the sand toward Maximilian's white Miramare Castle; but she'd never go into the water above her knees, and even when the wind was strong enough to flip the pages of her husband's book, only a few single hairs would slip from her braided chignon.

"They live on old money, the Hilgers," my father told me. "Inherited money from his grandfather. It's all invested in music stores."

Those first few days around them, I barely noticed Herr Hilger except when he did something for his wife, like open a door or drape her white jacket around her tanned shoulders, careful not to touch her bare skin. "*Lovely manners,*" my grandmother would have said about him. "*So attentive.*" But one afternoon, when he closed his book, a biography of Chopin, and kept it in his hands as if still thinking about it, I noticed his eyes—sea-green and melancholy—and I studied his face, wondering about the source of his sadness.

Frau Hilger took my hands into hers and extended them to her husband. "Look, Elmar—doesn't our Christa have the hands of a musician? Those long wrists and fingers?"

He set down his book. Crossed his arms. Nodded.

45

"You ought to let her read some of your biographies," she said. "You would like that, Christa, wouldn't you?"

I hesitated. The books I liked were Enid Blyton mysteries and sequels about two girls, Gisel and Ursel, who were good at sports. And the only music I listened to was *Schlager*—hits on the radio, many of them from America. Sometimes, when my best friend, Elsie, and I sang *Schlager*, we'd switch the words around but keep the melodies.

"Our Christa doesn't want to impose," Frau Hilger said. "You know how considerate she is."

"Of course," he said. "Any book you'd like to look at, Christa."

"He'll bring you one at dinner," she promised, but that evening it was she who handed me a biography of Verdi.

"I saw *Aïda* before Christa was born," my father told her. "I remember reading in the program that Verdi asked for the equivalent of a hundred thousand *Mark* before he wrote a single note for his opera. He received it too. And that was in the nineteenth century."

"How much would that be worth today?" she asked.

"Easily seven . . . eight hundred thousand *Mark*."

Herr Hilger pressed his lips together, as if offended that anyone could discuss music in terms of money.

"What is Verdi's music like?" I asked him.

He regarded me gravely. "You'll need to hear it to understand. But you can begin by reading about him."

I started the biography in bed and read on the beach during the following days, feeling quite grown-up. One night I dreamed that Herr Hilger was walking a white dog on the sidewalk outside my school and that I ran out to meet him; but when I woke up, I couldn't remember the rest.

A Woman's Perfume

In the meantime, Frau Hilger was dedicating herself to improving me. "Men don't need to be bothered with things like that," she told my father when she took me to the beauty parlor and decided on a hairstyle for me that "will lift out your features, Liebchen." I'd been wearing it Farah Diba–style—parted in the middle and pulled back low across my ears—but she persuaded me that feathered bangs and a layered cut would bring out my maturity. As I watched myself change in the mirror of the beauty parlor, I felt as though I'd finally left childhood behind.

She bought me pearl earrings, a white suit with a short jacket, white shorts, white sandals. "White is the best color for both of us," she whispered to me in the dressing room as she buttoned my blouse, and I felt startled by the sudden revulsion that flushed through my body and vanished before I could think about it. "Actually off-white," she was saying as she closed the last button, "a shade of cream that's whiter than cream. Pearl-colored, really." She insisted I needed underwear to go with my new clothes, and what she chose were not the pastel cotton panties my mother used to get me, but soft lace the hue of my skin. I liked the feel of nylons on my legs. Promised myself I'd never again wear knee stocking or socks.

Whenever my father offered to pay for the things she bought me, Frau Hilger would remind him how much this meant to her. "I never have the chance to mother a girl. Just for these few weeks . . . please, don't deny me that pleasure."

Both Hilgers spoke to me as if I were their age, and soon I noticed that my father treated me differently too—with a certain politeness, almost. He'd ask my opinion instead of just making plans for us. And he stopped calling me Kind—child. I was sure it had to do with the way I now dressed. We still played

47

tennis most mornings, but he didn't rush at the ball the way he used to, and I began to win against him. At times he seemed bewildered, and I'd catch him watching me as if not under-standing what was happening to us; but the expression would pass so quickly that I couldn't be certain it had even been there.

Frau Hilger liked to put one arm around me, squeeze me gently, and I'd smell her light perfume. One morning, when I told her I liked the scent, she said it was from Paris and took me to her bedroom. From the bureau next to the narrow bed, she picked up an amber bottle. With the glass stopper, she dabbed a few drops on my left wrist.

"Wear it for three hours before deciding if you like it."

"But I love it already," I told her.

And I did. I still do. Over the past thirty years—while Farah Diba gave the Shah his long-awaited son and three more chil-dren; while she stood tall with her tiara during his long-awaited coronation; while I studied music in Berlin; while I married and divorced and married and divorced once again—I've tried different perfumes, of course, but I've never found another scent that suits me. Still, I don't think of it as mine.

"It's a fine quality to be impetuous," Frau Hilger cautioned me as she closed the amber bottle. "But there are two occasions in a woman's life when she needs to wait with her opinion. One is her first time with a man. Unless she is very discreet, it changes her status in the world. With the wrong perfume, it doesn't help to be discreet. It's obvious, there for everyone to smell. Remember—never buy until you've tested it on your skin for at least three hours."

"Why three hours?"

"Because by then it has merged with your own scent. A

good perfume—not the cheap, heavy stuff that overwhelms—but a good perfume is different on every woman."

At dinner, I thrust my left wrist at my father and Herr Hilger. "Do I smell different from Frau Hilger?"

My father blinked. Glanced at Frau Hilger.

"We are wearing the same perfume," I explained.

Herr Hilger bent toward my arm and sniffed the air above it. His smooth hair was brushed away from his forehead and curved around the back of his ears.

"You still like it, then?" Frau Hilger asked me, and when I nodded, she pulled the amber bottle from her purse. "For you to keep. I have another one. But remember—it is a woman's perfume. . . . More than a hint of it would be unsuitable on a young girl."

My friend Elsie would be far more interested in my perfume than in what I'd brought home from Italy last summer—the large black scorpion I'd found in a vineyard. While my father had grabbed my arm—"Careful, Christa, those things can be deadly"—my mother had darted forward and caught the scorpion in her sun hat. On our balcony she'd drowned it in red wine—"You need alcohol to preserve it"—and impaled it on a hairpin so that I could bring it to my school. My biology teacher still had the scorpion, fastened to a rectangle of wood. Smelling of wine and dust and sun and decay, the scorpion had its pincers extended and its tail with the poisonous stinger curved forward across its back, as if about to grasp its victim and deliver that dangerous sting.

When we took walks through Trieste, I liked it if Herr Hilger stayed by my side, letting his wife go ahead with my father. He talked to me about music as if I were an adult, and I wished Elsie could see me with him. I understood him so much better than anyone else. Once Frau Hilger was no longer around to fill each of his silences with words, he came forward with his deep voice. When I asked him which composer he admired most, he told me about Ludwig van Beethoven, who'd kept writing his music after he had lost his hearing.

"But how could he . . . if he didn't hear the music he composed?"

"Oh, but he could feel it, Christa. He could."

He said this in such a way that I knew his own life must have been at least as mysterious and tragic as Beethoven's, and I longed for him to link his sturdy fingers through mine and tell me those secrets he wouldn't tell anyone else.

One morning a package arrived for me by airmail from one of the Hilgers' music stores. Inside was a portable record player and one single record. It had a glossy, night-blue jacket with the yellow emblem of the Deutsche Grammophon Gesellschaft and gold lettering:

Ludwig van Beethoven
EROICA
Sinfonie Nr.3 Es-dur op. 55
Dirigent:
FERENC FRICSAY
Berliner Philharmoniker

"I wanted you to hear the most beautiful symphony ever written," Herr Hilger said.

He and I listened to the *Eroica* on my balcony while my father and Frau Hilger took the train to Venice to photograph the mosaics in the Basilica di San Marco. Four times we listened to the *Eroica*, and when I told him, "Maybe each time people hear the *Eroica*, they do the listening that Beethoven couldn't do for himself," Herr Hilger nodded as if he'd just thought the very same thought. But then he added that Beethoven's hearing had quite likely still been all right while he'd worked on his early symphonies.

I hummed the opening passage when we sat down for dinner at our usual table in the dining room without my father and Frau Hilger, who wouldn't return from Venice until late that evening. We'd never see their photos of the mosaics, because their film had fallen into a canal, they would tell us.

That night, alone, as my hands followed the thin fabric of my new nightgown down my thighs and back up, I found myself in the soft place between my thighs, and I could hear the *Eroica* until my breath stopped and I fell back. Though I'd touched there before, it hadn't been like that, and the following night my hand went back there again, and to the music.

Whenever she heard me hum to myself, Frau Hilger would make sure to point out my talent for music, even if I was just humming that altered *Schlager* about Farah Diba that had been going around school before summer vacation. It followed the popular melody of "*Marina, Marina, Marina, du bist ja die Schönste der Welt. . . .*"

Farah Diba, Farah Diba, Farah Diba,
du bist ja die Schönste der Welt.
Gib dem Schah ein Söhnchen,
sonst fliegst du bald vom Thrönchen,
genau so wie Soraya. . . .

Farah Diba, Farah Diba, Farah Diba,
you are the most beautiful one in the world.
Give the Shah a little son,
otherwise you'll soon get kicked off the little throne,
just like Soraya. . . .

Soraya had been the Shah's previous wife, a sultry woman with the saddest movie-star eyes I'd ever seen. Until two years ago, we used to sing the same song about her: "*Soraya, Soraya, Soraya, du bist ja die Schönste der Welt. . . .*" Herr Hilger was a much better man than the Shah, who would have kicked Frau Hilger off his throne years ago for not producing a male heir. Frau Hilger couldn't even have a daughter. But a daughter didn't count anyhow with the Shah: his very first wife had given him a daughter. Unless he had a male heir, there would be no coronation for him, though he'd been the ruler of his country for nearly two decades. The more I tried not to hum that melody around the Hilgers—after all, I didn't want to remind them that they couldn't have children—the more that melody seemed to live inside my throat.

"What are the words to that?" Frau Hilger asked me one afternoon when all of us were climbing the stone steps of the Roman amphitheater.

"I forgot," I lied. "That's why I just hum it."

"Herr Hilger and I have been planning to go to Venice for a recital of Verdi arias. But since you have such a love for music, I want you to have my ticket. If your father doesn't mind, I'll keep him company here. Herr Hilger can take you to Venice on the train. I know he'll enjoy the recital much more with you." She glanced at my father.

Say yes, I wished. *Yes yes yes . . .*

A Woman's Perfume

He stroked his mustache.

"It's just a matinee," she said. "They'll be back before dark."

Finally he nodded.

Frau Hilger pulled me close. "You and Herr Hilger have music as a common interest. And that is something to be nurtured."

The day before the recital she bought me a pearl-white dress with a white-embroidered collar in a shop near the Piazza dell'Unità d'Italia, and the following morning I wore that dress when I sat next to Herr Hilger on the train to Venice. We started out early, because Frau Hilger insisted we plan enough time to see the Palazzo Ducale and take a gondola. On the train were three black-haired girls my age, who stared at my light hair and whispered to each other rapidly. When they started laughing, hands over their mouths, I felt bothered and glanced at Herr Hilger, but he was looking out of the window. All at once it occurred to me that I'd never seen him touch his wife's skin. What I wouldn't understand until many years later was his passion for the chaste, romantic love that is never consummated — not even with his wife.

Outside the Venice train station, he bought two nut sticks from one of the street vendors. With our teeth we pulled the sweet, glazed nuts from the thin skewers and chewed them as we walked toward the Canal Grande, the sun on our faces. Arched bridges took us across the network of smaller canals until we reached the Piazza San Marco, where an old woman in a black dress sold us maize. While I held the yellow kernels in my outstretched palms, waiting for the pigeons to come closer, Herr Hilger took photos of me.

"Try not to move, Christa," he said.

The pigeons' cooing was monotonous, seductive. When they landed on me, I wanted to shake them off, their wings, their beaks, their claws—they felt disgusting, tender where they rasped against my arms, my hair, my shoulders—yet I stood still for his camera. Five years earlier, I had stood in this same piazza with my parents, laughing and tossing maize to the pigeons. "Why don't we ever see pigeons out at night?" I had asked my mother, and she'd told me the old women took the pigeons home in their black shawls at dusk.

I told that story to Herr Hilger when we ate our lunch of *scaloppine di pollo* in the restaurant of an eight-hundred-year-old *palazzo*. Our table was by a window that opened out to a small side canal, where painted boats unloaded crates of fruits and vegetables.

"My mother said the old women let the pigeons loose again in the morning . . . to lure back the tourists so that the women can sell their maize."

"That means the pigeons keep the old women alive," he said, and smiled at me.

It was the first time I'd seen him smile. It changed his whole face, took away that tired and sad expression. And it was because of something I had said. His green eyes were lighter than usual, and I felt certain he would always be my friend from now on. I'd have two best friends, Elsie and him. I imagined him *leaning toward me . . . raising one hand to my face, and—*

"What is it, Christa?" he asked.

My fantasy had stopped, and I didn't know what was to come next, just as I didn't know that I would never see the Hilgers after that summer.

"Verdi abandoned music," he said. "Right after his wife and

54

two children died. For one entire year he did not compose. He was still a young man. Just think—what a loss it would have been. . . . His most significant works, *Aïda* and *Otello,* came decades later, *Aïda* when he was almost sixty, *Otello* when he was in his mid-seventies and everyone thought he had long since retired."

While he told me the story of *Aïda,* water gushed out intermittently from the sides of the buildings that lined the canal and merged with the gray waters of the canal. *"The length of a good flush,"* Elsie would say. I wanted to tell that to Herr Hilger, but I didn't because it would have been childish.

He ordered *zuppa inglese* for me, *biscotti* for himself. "Verdi is the only composer I know of who has my allergy," he confided when I offered him a taste of my rum-custard cake.

"What kind of allergy?"

"Certain foods make us itch."

"Really?"

"Anything with milk."

"Even cheese?"

"Cheese, ice cream . . . If I even just had one spoonful of your *zuppa inglese,* I'd get itchy all over."

"You can't have ice cream? Not ever?"

He shook his head. "Sometimes it gets so bad that my neck and arms are chafed from where I've scratched myself. My first piano teacher told me that Verdi's hands were sometimes raw. . . ."

I saw myself *covering his sore hands with clean white gauze . . . holding them in mine, waiting for them to heal while we listen to Verdi's music.*

Though he was silent, I knew by now that there were always

words beneath his silences, and I wasn't surprised when he said them aloud. "An entire island . . . Do you know there is an entire island for the dead here, Christa? It's called San Michele. There's something really beautiful about that."

I didn't know what to say.

"An island that belongs to the dead. And close by is another island, Burano, where lace is made. Fine, beautiful lace . . . much of it for bridal veils."

"I was there with my parents."

"Death and love so close together . . ."

I shivered. "My mother bought a lace tablecloth on Burano. We saw a bride and groom come out of a church. Both had very large noses."

Once again, Herr Hilger smiled his rare, splendid smile for me.

"I wondered what their children's noses would look like, but my mother said to be kind."

"You're already one of the kindest people I know, Christa."

"Really? Sometimes my parents say I'm selfish. And stubborn."

"That's not how I know you."

When we took a gondola to the gilded concert hall, oil slicks shimmered on the water and trembled as we passed through them. In the molten gray of the water, they adjusted themselves again, spreading into their original shapes.

"I'm so delighted that Christa appreciated Verdi," Frau Hilger told my father the next day, as we all headed to the market.

"It was the most perfect day of my life," I said.

My father raised his eyebrows.

But Frau Hilger patted my arm. "It means the world to Herr Hilger to share his love for music."

A Woman's Perfume

She walked ahead with my father, and the two of them chose *prosciutto* and *salametti,* pimento-stuffed olives, figs, slices of casaba melon, and almond macaroons for the picnic she was planning for us by the lighthouse. When I stopped to look at a necklace, the thin vendor in the red shirt, who'd sold me an enameled mirror for Elsie only a few days before, began his friendly barter, one hand already reaching for my hair.

"Half," he said, dangling the tiny multicolored glass beads in front of me. "My uncle make on Murano, island of glass. I sell you for half original price. You let me stroke sun in your hair again. . . ."

I laughed and glanced at my father, but he did not shake his head as he usually did. Frau Hilger's face was set into her red-red smile, and the air was hot, dusty. Around me all movement, all sound, had ceased, and I suddenly found it hard to breathe with the vendor's bright beads so close to my eyes. I turned toward Herr Hilger, waiting for him to stop all this, but his eyes were glinting as though he were the one ready to touch me, at last, and knew it was what I wanted too—as I did, as all of us must have known I did, collaborators forever in that one long moment before I gripped the vendor's brown hand and placed it on top of my head, letting his fingers sink into my hair, giving up part of myself to defy the three adults as much as to please them, and I wished I were already years away from what felt so terribly confusing, but then the weight of the necklace fell on my throat. I no longer recall who paid for the necklace and fastened it around my neck—all I know is that I couldn't bear it against my skin, that I slipped it off when we reached a fish seller's stand, and that, when I dropped it into a metal pail filled with slippery scales and heads, the familiar clamor of the market rose around me once more as if someone had flipped up a switch.

Stolen Chocolates

My first love has tripled in size. I didn't recognize him, though I noticed him when he entered the Greek restaurant, because the waiter replaced his armchair with a piano bench before he let him sit down. He was with a woman who wore apple-green silk and was heavy too, though not nearly his weight.

"Vera," he called out across the restaurant, and hoisted himself from the piano bench. His bulk drifted toward me as if carried by the scent of the exotic spices, surprisingly agile, fleshy hands leading.

I glanced behind me, searching for an escape or some other woman named Vera, though I know it's not a common name. All through school, I was the only Vera in my class.

"Vera, sweetie, it's me—Eddie," he said as if accustomed to identifying himself to people he hadn't seen in a long time. His suit looked expensive, made to order, and in the amber glow of the fringed ceiling lamps, his hair was blond and curly as ever.

"Eddie," I said, trying to reconcile this man with the image of the wiry boy I'd followed around the neighborhood at fourteen. I would wait at the end of his street for hours, heart pounding, just to get a glimpse of him, and when he finally started noticing me, he blotted all the questions and uncertainties I'd felt up to that day about my future. Whenever he helped me with my chores in my grandparents' grocery store, I rewarded him with stolen chocolates that we ate until we both felt as though we were about to explode.

"We will always be together," we said the afternoon he kissed me. "We will always be together," we promised each other in our letters for nearly half a year after his family moved to Cleveland.

"You look good, Vera. Real good." The voice was the same, though the fat had changed his features and stretched his skin so tightly that there wasn't space for a single wrinkle. "How long has it been?"

"Almost thirty years, Eddie."

"How's the food here?"

I felt ill at the thought of him squeezing anything else into that body. "I sold them the restaurant."

"It was yours?"

"No, no. I'm selling real estate now. The new owner, Mr. Fariopoulos, gave me a bonus—two hundred dollars' worth of meals."

"I hear their buffet is famous. All you can eat for twelve ninety-five."

"I usually just order a vegetarian dish."

"My first wife died seven years ago." He said it as if her death had been the result of being a vegetarian. He motioned to his table. "Bonnie over there—we got married the year after."

"Sorry about your first wife. And congratulations on—"

"I don't like weddings."

"Okay."

"But that's what we're in Albany for. Another wedding. My cousin's boy. Come, sit with us."

I hesitated.

"You're probably waiting for someone."

"Not really."

"No argument, then." One hand on my elbow, the other balancing my plate and wineglass, he led me toward his table like a trophy, his hips brushing dangerously close to other tables.

Certain that everyone was staring at us, I felt ashamed of my embarrassment to be seen with him.

He introduced me to his wife, Bonnie. "This is Vera." He beamed. "You know, the Vera of my youth." He made me sound mysterious and glamorous, and I wondered what he'd told his wife about me.

She tucked her handbag under her arm and greeted me with the cautious smile of heavy women who don't trust thin women. Her face had the natural look you can only achieve with skillful makeup.

Eddie sat down, his knees spread to accommodate his enormous thighs. "My cousin says you married a dentist."

"That was finished a long time ago."

"Sorry to hear that."

"Don't. I was ready."

"Any kids?"

"A daughter. She's at the University of New Hampshire."

"Good for you. Bonnie and I, we have our own pharmacy. In a mall. She handles the cosmetics and over-the-counter stuff, I get to count the pills." He laughed. "Amazing . . . Remember how I used to hate math?" He leaned over to his wife, one hand across his tie to keep it from falling into my glass. "Vera let me copy her homework."

"And you helped me in the store."

But he didn't hear me. He was frowning at my plate of egg-plant and rice. "I think I'll go for the buffet, Bonnie."

"Me too."

His enormous backside blocked out half the buffet table as he loaded up his plate. Oh, Eddie, I thought, Eddie, unable to continue my meal as I watched him eat silently, shoveling his food into his mouth at an alarming speed, giving shape to my deepest fears. To think I used to eat like that as a girl. To think I sometimes still longed to eat like that.

"How long are you staying in Albany, Eddie?" I asked, wishing he hadn't come back at all.

"Hold that question, Vera. I'll be right back." His breath had taken on the rich aroma of the food. Pushing the piano bench back, he headed for the buffet.

Bonnie only kept up with him for three trips, and then she sank into her chair, tiny beads of moisture between her perfect eyebrows; but Eddie kept returning for more, and with each bite he swallowed, I felt my stomach distend, harden.

It was on Eddie's fifth approach to the buffet that the owner of the restaurant, Mr. Fariopoulos stepped into his way. He was nearly a head shorter than Eddie, and he raised one lean hand and held it up in front of Eddie's chest to stop him. Without lowering his voice, he informed Eddie that he had eaten enough. "More than enough," Mr. Fariopoulos said.

His face purple-red, Eddie stood there like a boy caught stealing chocolates, and I felt his humiliation as though it were my own. Nearly everyone in the restaurant was watching him, except Bonnie, who was staring at the white tablecloth, her face rigid. Eddie opened his mouth—not to say something, but to breathe easier. He did not move—neither toward the buffet nor toward our table.

I had no idea what I was about to say when I got up and walked toward Eddie and Mr. Fariopoulos. My stomach was aching as if I'd eaten far too much, and my heart was beating as fiercely as all those times I'd waited for Eddie to appear in the door of his house.

I linked my arm through his and gave a nod to Mr. Fariopoulos. "I'm glad you've had a chance to meet my friend, Eddie."

"Vera—" Mr. Fariopoulos started.

"The menu," I asked, "what do you have printed next to the word 'buffet'? Is it 'all you can eat'? Or 'all we let you eat'?"

"You and your friends are always welcome here."

"All we let you eat?"

"All you can eat. You know that. But we can't afford to keep this place open if everyone eats like him."

"Then I'll be glad to put it back on the market for you."

"Vera," Eddie said, "you don't have to—"

"But I do," I said, and turned to Mr. Fariopoulos. "Tell me"—now I was going—"how many of your customers stop after the first trip to the buffet? Do you give them a discount? A doggie bag?"

It ended up with Mr. Fariopoulos apologizing to Eddie and telling him there would be no bill at all. In the parking lot, Eddie was rather quiet, and his hands felt cold when I grasped them to say goodbye, but Bonnie told me to visit them if I ever got to Cleveland. What I didn't expect was the dream I had that night, a wonderfully erotic dream about Eddie—not the way he used to look as a boy, when I'd suffered that first, glorious crush on him, but the way he was now. He drew me into his huge embrace, sheltered me against his solid chest. We were lying in the meadow behind my grandparents' store, and spread in front of us were all the pastries and cakes I had ever denied myself. We ate together—passionately, joyfully—letting each other taste the most satisfying delicacies without remorse. Eddie's breath was sweet as he consumed me with his hungry mouth, replenished me with his hungry mouth. My arms were long enough to reach around him. His body felt light as he enveloped me into his soft vastness, so light that he took us all the way up to the sky.

Doves

Francine is having a shy day, the kind of day that makes you feel sad when the elevator man says good afternoon, the kind of day that makes you want to buy two doves.

Her raincoat pulled around herself, Francine walks the twelve blocks to Portland Pet and Plant. She heads past the African violets, past the jade plants and fig trees, past the schnauzers and poodles, past the hamsters and turtles, past the gaudy parrot in the center cage who shrieks: Oh amigo oh amigo . . .

What Francine wants are doves of such a smooth gray that they don't hurt your eyes. With doves like that you don't have to worry about being too quiet: they'll make soft clucking sounds deep inside their throats; they'll turn their heads toward the door when you push the key into the lock late in the afternoon; they'll wait for you to notice them instead of clamoring for your attention.

And she finds them—doves just like that, six of them—perched in a cage near the back wall with a sign above it: *Ring Neck Doves $7.99.* Two are white with brownish speckles, the others a deep gray tinged with purple.

Oh amigo oh amigo . . . screeches the parrot.

Doves

❦   ❦   ❦

Francine chooses the two smallest gray doves and carries them from the pet shop in cardboard boxes that look like take-out Chinese with air holes. The afternoon smells like damp newspaper, but she feels light as she walks back to her apartment. In her kitchen she sets the white boxes on her counter, opens them, and waits for the doves to fly out and roost on the plastic bar where she hangs her kitchen towels. But they crouch inside the boxes as if waiting for her to lift them out.

She switches on the radio to the station where she always keeps it, public radio, but instead of Tuesday-evening opera, a man is asking for donations. Francine has already sent in thirty-six dollars, and she doesn't like it when the man says: None of you would think of going into a store and taking something off the shelves, but you listen to public radio without paying. . . .

The doves move their wing feathers forward and pull their heads into their necks to shield themselves from the fund-raising voice. Francine turns the dial past rock stations and commercials. At the gaudy twang of a country-western, the doves raise their heads and peer from the boxes. Their beaks turn to one side, then to the other, completing a nearly full circle. Low velvet sounds rise from their throats. Francine has never listened to country-westerns—she's considered them tacky—but when the husky voice of a woman sings of wanting back the lover who hurt her so, Francine tilts her head and croons along with the doves.

In the morning, before she leaves for her job at Kmart, Francine pulls the radio next to the kitchen sink and turns it on for the doves, who've settled themselves in the left basin of her double

65

sink, their claws curled around folds of the yellow towel she's spread in the basin, their eyes on the tuner that still flickers on the country-western station. When she returns after working all day in the footwear department, they swivel their heads toward her and then back to the radio, as if they'd been practicing that movement all day.

At Kmart, she finds that more and more people leave their shoes. It used to be just once or twice a week that she'd discover a worn pair of shoes pushed under the racks by someone who walked away in stolen footwear. But now she sees them almost every day—sneakers with torn insoles, pumps with imitation leather peeling from the high heels, work shoes with busted seams—as if a legion of shoe thieves had descended on Portland.

Francine saves the discarded shoes in the store's lost-and-found crate, though no one has ever tried to claim them. But some are still good enough to donate to Goodwill. She murmurs to the doves about those shoe thieves while she refills their water and sprinkles birdseed into the porcelain soap dish. Coming home to them has become familiar. So have the sad songs of lost love that welcome her every evening. A few times she tried to return to public radio, but as soon as the doves grew listless, she moved the tuner back. And lately she hasn't felt like changing it at all. She knows some of the lines now, knows how the songs end.

Francine has a subscription to the opera—a birthday present she gives herself every September. After feeding the doves, she takes a bubble bath and puts on her black dress. In back of the cab, she holds her purse with both hands in her lap. Sitting in the darkened balcony, she feels invisible as she listens to *La Traviata*. For the first time it comes to her that, just like the country songs, this too is about lost love.

In the flood of bodies that swells from the opera house, Francine walks into the mild November night, leaving behind the waiting cabs, the restaurants, the stores. From a small tavern, a couple saunters hand in hand, steeped in amber light and the sad lyrics of a slow-moving song for just that one instant before the door will close once again. But Francine won't let it. Francine curves her fingers around the doorknob, pulls at it, and steps into the smoky bar as if she were a woman with red boots who had someone waiting for her. Below the Michelob clock, on a platform, two men are playing guitars and singing of betrayed love.

On the bar stool, Francine's black dress rides up to her knees. She tugs at her hem, draws her shoulders around herself, and orders a fuzzy navel. It's a drink she remembers from a late-night movie, and it tastes just the way she imagined it would—of summer and apricots and oranges—soothing her limbs, opening her shoulders.

A lean-hipped man asks her to dance, and as she sways in his arms on the floor that's spun of sawdust and boot prints, she becomes the woman in every song that the men on the platform sing: the woman who leaves them; the woman who keeps breaking their hearts.

Freitod

Sabine Dönstetter sits in the warm sand above the high-water mark, looking out over the conflicting currents, which are so strong here at the end of the Baja that you can count on being swept out to sea. Waves leave tongues of foam on the beach as the water retreats; an intricate pattern of tiny craters remains in the sand, and through them bubbles surge up to fill the hollows.

A tangled piece of seaweed lies crusted next to Sabine's bare feet. Old-woman feet, she thinks, and brushes specks of sand from her ankles. Her first day in Mexico, her legs were bitten by sand fleas. It seems only moments ago that these same legs belonged to the girl who ran along the island beaches of Rügen, kicking up sprays of salty water. Sabine pictures her son, Horst, arriving from Berlin at the Los Cabos airport in his business suit, riding one of the vans to the hotel in Cabo San Lucas, and standing on the terrace of the restaurant with Armando, the stocky waiter with the melodious voice, who serves Sabine papaya juice every morning.

Armando will point across the waves of the Pacific. "*La*

señora, su madre," he says to Horst, "she looked at the waves for many hours. We spoke about *la señora.*"

Armando enjoys teasing Sabine about buying her watch from her—a parody of the barter between tourists and the vendors who sell jewelry, blankets, and pottery in the market near the ferry landing. "How much you want for your watch?" Armando will ask Sabine, and when she tells him she doesn't want to sell it, he smiles and insists, "I'll give you good price. . . . Almost new . . . Cheap, I buy it cheap."

She doubts that Armando will engage Horst in his banter. *They're both serious as they stand on the terrace where palm trees grow, their nuts nestled where the trunk meets the leafy branches, pulled in like testicles on a freezing man. One of the slight amber cats that swarm around the hotel brushes past Horst's legs, almost touching. A fishing boat moves fast and parallel to shore. Warm air carries the scent of the hibiscus blossoms that grow between the hotel and the sand-colored rocks. Those rocks have rounded holes in them like Picasso sculptures, and they turn pink at sunset. On the way to his room, Horst runs one hand across a rock and finds a shell wedged into one of the smooth crevices.*

Sabine feels the wind on her neck, a strong wind that moves across the ocean, making it look like a river; yet the waves keep crashing in. Where the sky meets the sea, it is hazy but fans into brilliant blue toward the December sun. A streak of water shoots up as though something had been dropped from a great height, and the arched body of a whale surfaces for an instant— black against the gray of the ocean.

Sabine has been planning this day of her death, much in

the way as she planned the day of her wedding forty-eight years ago—with the kind of momentum that makes it impossible to stop. Then, she began sewing her wedding dress the day Werner proposed to her. Six months ago, on her way home from the doctor's office, she stopped at a travel agency where she booked this trip to what she calls the end of Mexico because she knew she didn't want to walk into the freezing Ostsee, knew she wanted that last submersion to be kind. At a department store she chose a swimsuit that matched the vibrant colors in the travel brochures.

Sabine doesn't regret leaving life. Only that she has to disguise it as an accident. Because of the laws, for one—you can get yourself locked up if you fail. And then, of course, her children. She thought the hardest part would be making the choice, but it isn't. Even in her dying she is worried about her children. She doesn't want them to feel responsible, doesn't want to encumber them with her body to take home and abandon to the craft of the undertakers. In Germany, there are two words for what she is about to do: *Freitod*—free death, and *Selbstmord*—murder of the self. And what she is choosing is *Freitod*.

"A terrible accident," Armando will tell Horst, "such a misfortune."

Horst will stay for the night. *At breakfast he sits at the table where Sabine used to eat, near the retired insurance man from America and his wife who come here for three weeks every winter. The husband orders a fruit plate for his wife, oatmeal for himself. Instead of stirring the oatmeal, he draws up his spoon to eye level and lets the gray, lumpy matter dribble back down. His wife— lips pressed together—watches, looking unhappy in her pink sun-*

dress. When her husband finally eats, he opens his mouth long before the spoon gets there; his tongue darts out, the spoon trembles, and then he traps the spoon inside his wide mouth.

When the insurance man offers his condolences to Horst, he tells him that people don't swim on the Pacific side; they swim in the Sea of Cortés. And Horst returns to Berlin reassured that it was an accident—that his mother was careless, perhaps even stubborn to attempt swimming in the rough Pacific, where the waves don't flatten themselves against the shore but slam from a great height before they get sucked out to sea as if by greater force.

He tells his sister, Inge, about the doctor from Holland who came here to fish for marlin and broke three ribs when the waves slammed him against the sand. Armando had to haul him in a wheelbarrow across the vast beach and through the lobby to the circular drive, where the ambulance picked him up. Horst tells Inge about the signs along the beach that warn swimmers of the riptide—water agitated by conflicting tides or currents—and they grieve as children grieve for their parents, not nearly as deeply as a parent will grieve for a child.

Because that is the nature of being a parent, Sabine has discovered. You love your children far more than you ever loved your parents, and—in that love, and in the recognition that your own children cannot fathom the depth of your love—you come to understand the tragic, unrequited love of your own parents.

A pattern of tire tracks stretches along the length of beach. Last night Sabine heard one of the fat-wheeled, motorized tricycles pass her hotel and return an hour later. The sand is pale where she sits but looks darker, heavier the closer it gets to the ocean.

She has been in Cabo San Lucas for one week. She has tasted the most fabulous cheese pie sold by local women at the ferry landing; has slept deeply without anything between her skin and the night air; has walked beneath the beauty of the vultures and the stars; has watched sleek surfers in glistening rubber suits return from the sea.

She has felt embarrassed by three German tourists she overheard while on an excursion boat, complaining loudly—as though no one else could possibly understand their language—about the Mexican food. "At least we still have some good German booze," one of them said, startled as Sabine turned around and reminded them in German that they were guests in this country.

It has been a week of colors, a week to test her choice and let herself return to Berlin if that is what she decides. Ever since that afternoon in the doctor's office, when he wanted to schedule her for surgery, Sabine has felt as if everything around her has snapped into focus, the colors brighter, the shapes clearer. It makes her regret not always having seen like this. And even the pain—which keeps growing heavier, as though a sharp-fanged animal were trying to gouge its way from her belly—has not been able to take from her that sense of everything happening for the first time.

Sabine has always known when to end what doesn't work before it becomes unbearable. Like her marriage when she was forty-two. It could have gone on in the same way, becoming increasingly silent until the only sound would have been that of her breath while she lay next to Werner, unable to sleep.

She has friends who waited beyond the time when they could have chosen to leave life. The day before she left Berlin,

Freitod

she said goodbye to her friend Ulrike Heuss—two years younger than she—who has periods of forgetfulness and cries with shame whenever she wets her bed in the nursing home, where an activity director and a nutritionist make decisions for her. Sabine doesn't know which is worse: the trained staff of a nursing home or the concern of her children.

"Any time you want to move in with us . . .," her daughter has offered more than once.

"You know you're always welcome to live with me," her son has assured her.

They're both protective. Puzzled by her determination to look after herself, they've told her it forces them to worry even more about her.

Sabine looks at the insect bites on her thighs, traces them with her fingers up to her colorful swimsuit. Ah, she tells herself, but I am a woman who had a lover. Her lover was with her that night when she first encountered the death that has been waiting for her ever since.

They were the only ones camping in the vast canyon above a creek that flowed from one basin to the next, connected by waterfalls. Their fire flickered, casting shadows of long-gone generations against the stone walls on the other side of the canyon. The night was warm, and after loving, they walked down to the largest of the basins. At its far end, streaks of water cascaded, reminding Sabine of pictures she'd seen of Hawaiian women standing beneath warm waterfalls, hands raised to their long hair, fanning it out, while luminous beads envelop them.

But as she entered the basin, a current pushed outward

from the waterfall, and she had to pull herself along the cliff to get beneath it. Instantly, the force of the water drummed down on her, pushed her beneath its churning surface, and as she struggled to surface, she screamed out. Her lover waved to her and laughed as though they were playing a game, but when she went under again and emerged with louder screams, his expression changed to panic and he kept running into the water and backing up because he didn't know how to swim. And as the pressure of the waterfall pushed her down, down, Sabine thought how ridiculous it was that the water she loved would cause her death, and she had another thought then, very clearly—that her death would come to her in water, but that now was too soon. She felt calm, almost at home in that silver womb, and it was with something close to regret that she sought for a foothold on the slippery rock wall, pushed both feet against it, and catapulted herself away, shooting out below the water's embrace. As she surfaced outside its coil, outside that ring of tension that surrounded the waterfall where it hit the basin, she was trembling—not from fear, but because she was no longer afraid of death.

From that night forward, she would think of the canyon as dividing her life into before and after.

It is late afternoon, long after the excursion boats have returned to the harbor, after the fishing boats have pulled in their marlins and tunas and dolphins. Sabine takes off her watch, leaves it on a flat stone for Armando to find. Dark-gray crabs move across the beach like tumbleweeds, and as she walks toward the ocean, the crabs bury themselves in the sand as if pulled into vortexes, leaving penis-shaped holes and half-fans of sand that look like the raised imprints of shells.

Four pelicans ride the crests close to shore. One of them lifts itself off, feet brushing the water for an instant. Sabine brings herself to the edge of the sea, gently. Frothy salt water swirls around her calves. She waits for a large wave and slides into its backwash as it is sucked out, drawing her along without judgment, without refusal. Swimming steadily, she dives below the crests that seek the shore.

The body that has become such a burden to her feels light as she heads out, her back to the peninsula. If she wants to, she can imagine there's no land in sight, no place to return to once her arms and legs get too tired to keep her afloat. But why not accept the solid sand behind her and, despite its safety, choose the open expanse of water and sky? She swims, her eyes on the horizon, yet knowing the line of the shore and the rock ledges that become smaller and more urgent where Baja ends and the Pacific merges with the Sea of Cortés.

Moonwalkers

My father has the heart of a twenty-seven-year-old woman. While waiting for a transplant, he didn't worry about the donor, because he forced all his strength into willing his own heart to endure long enough. But now he speaks about her as though she were still alive.

"She is studying to be a librarian," he whispers to me when I arrive at the hospital, where he lies hooked up to tubes and monitors. The puckered skin beneath his chin stretches, tissue-thin.

Beyond his window, the sky is streaked with the blues of dusk; but inside, the lights are as white as the sheets and walls, sealing my father from all that lies out there, from time past and time yet to be. He seems oblivious to the noise around him: machines beeping; wheelchairs clattering; people shouting; televisions droning.

"Reading . . . She is constantly reading. Her parents . . ."

As he raises both hands toward me, I'm once again alarmed by how uncertain they've become, how brittle. Only a year ago, when he retired from his physical-therapy practice and surprised my wife, Eleanor, and me with a visit, his hands were still rugged. He helped us rake the fallen leaves behind the house, caulk the skylight in our sunroom. He has always relied on his hands—their knowledge, their wisdom—more than he relied on sight. But now he's maneuvering through uncharted territory. "She is two months younger than you," he tells me.

Smells of iodine and cleansers and gladiolas clash in his cold room. Two gurneys rumble past his open door, harsh against the tiles. White sheets cover the patients to their chins, and I wish I could follow them—away from my father. Instead, I sit down on the edge of his bed. Stroke his wrist with two fingers. Trace the plastic bracelet with his name. My name. John Bauer. His name used to be Hans, but he changed it to John when he emigrated from Austria as a young man. For him, touch has always been easy, part of his work. But for me, it's not easy to be near my father. I feel ashamed for noticing, ashamed for not being a more compassionate son. But touching my father shrinks the distance between us too much. Will I still be able to say no to him now that he is frail? *No, I cannot take off from work to go hiking with you. No, I cannot call you back in five minutes. No, I—*

"She carries books with her wherever she . . ." His head lolls to the side, and his eyes follow the arc of the branches. This time of year is his favorite, the leaves still full while starting to turn red or golden.

I try not to notice the flaky skin on his scalp. Against the pillow, his baldness is almost aggressive. Though he had no hair left when I started my junior year, I rarely saw him without a hairpiece so well crafted it could pass for real. By the time I graduated from high school, I had my own bald spot, and it has widened since, the way snow gives way to piss in a nearly perfect circle. I have promised myself two things: to never wear a hair-piece, and to never comb my few remaining hairs sideways across my bald spot.

My cousin, Nick, still brushes his hair like that, long blond wisps that flop in the wind and make Nick look even balder than he is. The day before my graduation, he and I split the cost of an aerosol spray that was guaranteed to camouflage hair loss. It came in three colors—black, brown, beige—and we picked beige because that was close enough for both of us. When we sprayed the backs of each other's heads, it fizzed like shaving cream but smelled like wet paint. Most of it stayed on my pillow that night, and the rest ended up on my graduation robe like a drastic case of dandruff.

My father's fingers are bone. Ice. I grip them. Because I want to be here for him. I do. For as long as I can remember, I have fought to extricate myself from him, while at the same time being tugged toward him. In college, I didn't answer most of his letters and phone calls. Once I lived away from him, the words we used to move back and forth between us no longer fit. And yet I found some balance—an uneasy balance—in being cut off from him and yet linked. Safe. Because I knew he would take the first step toward me again. And again.

I don't have that kind of courage. And I feel embarrassed by people who do. Embarrassed by their naked urgency. When-ever I feel ignored by Eleanor because she's reading or playing computer games, I retreat. Because I'm afraid of what I really want: to cling to her. And I'm afraid of disgusting her with my devotion. My father's devotion was too much for me alone. I never was enough for him, and I used to wish he had more children. Perhaps then his marriage to my mother would have lasted. There was the almost-child, a girl, who'd died after five months in my mother's womb, a stay long enough to settle her in my father's plans for his future years, plans that then shifted to me when I was born, making the absence of that child my loss. My duty: to replace her with my body; to multiply my love.

" . . . two months younger . . ." My father's eyelids flutter, bluish, half transparent.

I pull the blanket to his shoulders, tuck the musty-smelling sheet loosely around his chin. "You want me to get you another blanket?"

"Step back," he says urgently.

"What is it?"

"She should step back."

He must be talking about his donor. From his doctor I know she was standing on a sidewalk in downtown Portland when a motorcycle jumped the curb and struck her. Only her heart has survived, beating inside my father, who is prepared to treat it responsibly. Over the past months, he has grown thin, the kind of thin that comes with waiting. He has never been good at waiting, taught me that waiting was a weakness. Each time he visits Eleanor and me in Lincoln City, he is impatient to return to the mountains of Joseph, where he settled forty years ago because the landscape reminded him of the Austrian Alps. He loved to climb up the steep paths of the Wallowas or down into Hells Canyon to the Snake River, and by the time I was six, he took me along, encouraging me to keep moving forward whenever I thought I could not take another step. "Challenge yourself, John," he would say.

My wife says it's cruel to constantly push a child. Although some days I agree with Eleanor, I do believe that, without my father, I wouldn't understand what lies beyond that first barrier where most of us give up. Or the next barrier. By nature, I'm lazy. Extraordinarily lazy. It's just that I haven't tested that laziness. Not yet. Because of my father.

Eleanor says she can't imagine me lazy. But I know my capacity, know that what saves me, even today, is how on those mountain paths I learned to set one foot ahead, then the other, until eventually my father would let me rest and point back at the additional stretch I'd walked. "Aren't you glad I made you challenge yourself?" he'd ask, and start pulling nuts and raisins and oranges from his leather backpack. While we'd eat, I'd feel content. Proud even. He'd tell me the names of flowers and of birds, so pleased when I'd remember their names from previous hikes. Some days we'd glimpse deer far away. Vermin, my father called them. But I loved watching their movements—like sudden light on water.

The windowpanes vibrate as a helicopter takes off from the roof of the hospital. When my father lifts his head, his throat emerges—gray and sharp—from the nest of sheet I've spun around him.

"I want to meet her parents. They—" Though he's moving his lips, I can't hear the rest of what he's saying over the roar of the helicopter.

Last night, before Eleanor and I left here, Dr. Meyer took me aside. He's concerned my father is getting too enmeshed in the donor's life. "Or death, rather," he said.

"But how can he not?" I asked. "You won't tell him her

name, just a few details like her age and her profession . . . what she liked to do and how she died."

"Sometimes grief makes people really crazy," Dr. Meyer said. "Sometimes they are crazy anyway. And then it's better for the recipient to stay anonymous."

Still, my father continues to ask about her parents. I think they want to mourn their daughter—not adopt some man who is a generation ahead of her. I see her *lying on a metal table after her brain death has been established, still hooked up to machines that breathe for her, that keep fluids and blood salts in balance, until her heart is harvested for my father.*

Harvested.

That's what it's called, according to Dr. Meyer. *A harvest of hearts. Of kidneys. And livers. Of eyes and toes and spleens and ears and—Stop it. A cannibalistic feast. Stop—*

"Dr. Meyer told me you're doing well," I say quickly. The skin on my face feels dry and stretched from two hours in the car to Portland. I bend across my father. "Really well."

He smells of mouthwash and, oddly, gladiolas, even though there are no gladiolas in his room. Just roses. Two bouquets of roses from Eleanor and me. But those I can't smell. Just those gladiolas. *Funeral flowers. A scent from the future?*

No. Stop it now—

How to grieve when you don't know the language of grief?

My mother spoke the language of grief, carried it in her gaunt body where the almost-child had lived and died. That grief was all she had left. Her tears dried up entirely, and her eyes felt hot. When she put in drops to soothe them, her sight shimmered as though she were looking up from the bottom of a pond.

Ten years it took my mother—ten years and two months—to become pregnant with me, as though her body were denying her passage of another child. Perhaps she could have shed her grief if she hadn't let my father claim me so entirely as his. Whenever I think of my parents during my early years, I feel I'm seeing them through binoculars: my father enlarged, right up against my face; my mother reduced, fading from me while I watch her through the wrong end of the binoculars.

I don't even know the words for grief.

How to grieve when you don't know the language of grief?

"Dr. Meyer . . . he talked with her parents," my father is saying. His features are jagged, small. He has no flesh left to waste. Not much between himself and death.

But he is recuperating, I tell myself. He's not dying. Soon he'll get out of the hospital, and he'll only return to have his knees and hips repaired to match his youthful heart, to hike faster and higher than I ever will, to beat me at tennis, at everything I have tried and will try.

"You'll feel much better," I say. "Once you get out of here and back into your own house."

"She reads a lot, John. She . . ."

I can feel the fusion between the donor and my father—their only language the murmur of blood—and for an instant I feel left out. Envious. She has taken the space of the almost-child, the daughter who will release me from his aspirations. *What does that make her relationship to me, then?*

" . . . has at least a dozen novels on her night table, some just started, some almost finished. Maybe Dr. Meyer can ask her parents if they'll let me borrow the books. . . ."

In the room next door a woman and a man are arguing loudly above the television laughter.

" . . . she hasn't finished yet . . . so I can read those books for her." That moment, somehow, my father feels closer to me in age. More contained. How much has the heart of this woman changed who he is? Is that even possible?

"You and books?" I tease him. Because he's not much of a reader, my father. He has tried to blame it on being an immigrant. All he reads are professional journals and *The Oregonian*. While my mother would vanish into a book for days, emerging only to teach her Spanish classes at the high school or to go to the library for more books.

"Me and books," he says without hesitation. "Bugs."

"Books?"

He starts swatting at his head. "Bugs. Bugs in here."

"There are no bugs here."

Trailing tubes and wires, his hands ambush his ears and his neck, like frenzied birds. "Bugs in here . . ."

"I promise you there are no bugs in here."

But he's whimpering. "John—"

"All right. Let me get the bugs off you." I sweep my fingers across his face, his dry skull. Pluck away imaginary bugs. Step on them.

"Bugs . . ."

"All gone." I capture his hands in flight. "See? They're all gone."

"Step back." He struggles to sit up. "Step—"

"The bugs are all gone now, Dad. I squashed them all." I try to think of something to distract him. "Hey, you want to hear something funny?"

He frowns. "Funny . . ." A single bead of sweat sits between his eyebrows.

"You want to hear something funny?"

"Funny . . . Yes . . ."

"One night last week, when I came home from installing a security system in Neskowin, I found two messages on my machine. A woman's voice: 'This is Mrs. Lodge from Tiffany's school. She said you were going to pick her up, but since we haven't heard from you, we'll simply put her on the bus.' Click."

It's the kind of story my father would usually get into, plant his opinions, insist it would be best for Tiffany to live with the dependable Mrs. Lodge from now on. *"Parents who forget their children don't deserve their children," he would say. "And parents who name a child Tiffany don't deserve being parents." He'd grimace as he'd say "Tiffany." "I've never met a Tiffany who wasn't a brat. Such a goddamn precious name. Expensive, exclusive, privileged . . ." He'd speculate about the names of Tiffany's brothers and sisters: "Brittany . . . Cameron . . ."*

Instead, he lies there silently, hands twitching in mine as he pursues hallucinatory bugs. I miss his odd humor, even though it has brought him trouble. Just a few months before he retired, a forty-four-year-old patient, Vicky Cotter, threatened to sue him for unprofessional conduct. She was referred to him because of pains in her upper back, and while my father was massaging her shoulders, she moaned and told him she already felt much better. My father laughed and said what I'm sure he's said to a hundred other female patients before: "I know it takes a lot to keep you old gals going." He still calls his receptionist and assistant "the girls." Teases his patients that they just want to lie there all day and have their backs rubbed. Had he been born into this country thirty years later, he would have automatically picked up the appropriate words. What happened, though, is that the dislocation from his first language was all he could bear. Once he settled within his second language, he ignored all nuances of change. Though most of his patients enjoy his bantering, others have climbed off his massage table and left. Like Vicky Cotter, who fortunately did not follow up on her threat to sue him.

I stroke the backs of my father's hands, the raised veins, the creased valleys between them. "The same woman's voice was on the next message too, Dad. Very agitated. 'Hello, this is Mrs. Lodge from Tiffany's school again. Hello—'"

"Hello," my father echoes. "Hello . . ."

"'Hello, are you there? We reconsidered and decided to keep Tiffany here at school until you can pick her up.'"

"Children . . ."

"Do you think Mrs. Lodge ever realized she had the wrong number?"

He coughs. Winces.

"Daddy?"

His body is shaking with each cough. "Those stitches—"

I slip my palm beneath his neck. "Daddy?" Lift his head off the pillow till he stops coughing. "You want me to get the nurse?"

"No." He takes a careful breath. Another. As though he were learning to breathe all over again. "Not the nurse. She says I'll die twitching . . . because of the rabbits. Patients who eat rabbits will die twitching."

"I can't believe anyone would say that."

"I only ate rabbits in Austria, John . . . never in America."

"If she said that, she didn't mean it." Cautiously, I guide his head back down. His pillow feels too rough for his brittle skin. "And you're not going to die. You hear me?"

"Children . . . You should . . ." His voice trails off.

Music from a car radio comes closer, booms, fades. It's still warm enough to drive around with open windows.

"Listen to that," my father says. "You and Nick—you tooled around like that. I used to wish I . . ."

"In Austria—did you tool around in Austria?"

"Something to do for kids in America. We . . . were men when we were fourteen. Not boys . . . like you. And we didn't have cars . . . like here."

When I was in high school, we'd cruise up and down the few familiar blocks through town every Friday night, take a U-turn, and loop back. Joseph, Oregon, was bordered by the immense Wallowas, which kept us there. The highway, however, suggested a world beyond. As we cruised—the girls three or four to a vehicle, the boys alone—we'd approach and pass each other again and again, glancing around with practiced aloofness as we posed in our souped-up trucks and cars. My cousin, Nick, who was blond and tanned quickly even in winter, painted his truck bright yellow, as if to transmit the colors of his body to the outside. Some vehicles would stop along the side of the street, where we'd sit on the hoods, watching this parade of our own making that we'd been getting ready for all week—the boys in jeans and T-shirts with the name of a rock band; the girls in shorts and tops with spaghetti straps. Uniforms, of sorts.

Since we all went to the same school, we knew exactly how each of us was pegged—popular or not-so-popular—and while those ratings still defined us, there was a chance that they might change on Friday nights: because a popular girl might climb from her friends' car into a boy's vehicle and elevate his rating forever; because a boy might suddenly lean from his truck window to look into the eyes of a not-so-popular girl and make her desirable from that day forward.

My mother once said our cruising reminded her of a ritual she'd seen as a student teacher in a Mexican village, where the young women would stroll around the fountain in a plaza after dusk, scrutinized by the young men who leaned against the columns of the promenade. Our cruising ritual, she said, was not all that different, except that we could be anonymous, protected by metal and glass, by the speed at which our cars moved, by the blaring music that made it possible to ignore comments we might not want to hear.

"Listen . . ." my father says again, long after the car radio has faded.

"Yes?"

"I think you should . . ." He looks immeasurably sad.

I try to cheer him. "Do you think Mrs. Lodge still has Tiffany with her? A week after those phone messages?"

"I think . . . you should have children, John." At least he's no longer talking about bugs.

"I'm too young, Dad."

"It's the most important thing . . . I've done in . . . my life."

Too important. But of course I can't say that aloud.

"I would have called that . . . Mrs. Lodge."

"But I didn't know from which school she—"

"I would have found out."

"I believe you."

When I was three years old, he started taking me to his office occasionally, where I enjoyed playing on the floor next to the receptionist's desk while he was in a room, working on patients. By the time I was in preschool, he'd reschedule or cancel appointments to attend conferences with my teacher. The same, later, with grade-school conferences, with high-school plays and concerts. At home he'd quiz me about my classes, check my homework late at night, discuss with me what he allowed me to watch on TV.

The women I dated before Eleanor used to envy me for having him as a father. "He's so supportive of everything you do," they'd say.

"Too supportive," I'd answer.

But they'd still go on. "And he's totally devoted to you."

I'd nod. "Oh, yes, totally."

What I first loved about Eleanor was that she told me, "Your father holds on to you too much."

My mother used to sit with me when I did my homework, but the more my father nested himself in my life, the more she receded. Until he had taken so much of me that there was nothing left for her. It was then that she started feeding the deer, luring them close to our house with apples and buds and acorns and twigs. Closer yet with salt blocks for them to lick. At first, they approached cautiously, stiffly; but soon they romped through our garden as if it were their domain.

"Did you know," my mother said to me, "that deer need at least six pounds of feed a day to last through the winter?"

"Did you know," my mother said, "that if a pregnant doe gets too thin she'll absorb her unborn?"

"Did you know," she said. "that she turns it back into being part of herself?"

Up close, my mother's deer were mangy—matted fur;

patches of scabbed hide—and I wished I'd only seen them from a distance, where they'd been lithe and graceful.

My wife says I do better with everyone at a distance, not just deer. "It's where you've placed your father. Your mother too, though not that much. It's what you do with your clients."

"It's my clients who want the distance," I remind her. I install security systems for the summer people who built immense houses that encroach on the marshes and ponds of the Oregon coast, on the streams and ocean, endangering the animals that are forced from their habitats. The larger the body of water, the more flagrant the house, and the more exorbitant the system to keep it protected.

"I won't let you place me at that distance," Eleanor likes to tell me. She is a fierce fighter, my wife. Fights as easily and passionately as she laughs. Even fights me when I refer to her as my wife. Protests that it sounds like one word: *mywife*. To bait her, I sometimes call her that when we make love. *Mywife*. Until she presses her knuckles against my ribs or tickles me.

"What's it worth to you?" she'll ask if I beg her to stop. "What's it worth to you, John?"

"You'll get to climax first next time."

"The two next times."

My father is watching the sky get darker, turning purple. The trees are no longer three-dimensional, just black cardboard cutouts. Without depth. All one.

When he forbade my mother to feed the deer—"your goddamn vermin," he said—she moved into the house of her friend Helen, the art teacher at the high school where my mother taught. Since my father didn't want to admit that she'd left him, he told our neighbors he was sending her away because she was letting the deer destroy our perennials.

My mother's tears returned to her once she lived in Helen's house by the edge of the forest, where deer came to her readily, and where I stayed with her during the week. The lens of the binoculars flipped. Set her into proportion. She grew taller, wider. Even her voice became fuller.

It was easy to breathe inside her house. But Friday evenings my father would claim me, challenging me to do better, yet undoing my accomplishments by reminding me he was the one who'd urged me to do better: paint the fence in one day; get an A on a science test; swim twenty laps in our pool. . . . I try not to do that to others—make their accomplishments mine. Or force them to my will. The way my father did with that pool. How I hated that pool. He and I dug it together after my mother left. I was eleven, and he pushed me past blisters, past tears, past tiredness, telling me how those things that were the hardest for us allowed us to live the rest of our lives with ease.

That first night he and I used the pool, the underwater light turned the water a transparent green, tracing the dark shapes of our arms and legs with tiny bubbles. The water felt like velvet, and our movements seemed slower than during the day. And I thought that maybe my father was right, that the easy part of my life was starting.

But the following morning, I found him crouching by the side of the pool as though he'd dropped something into the water. He pointed to the surface, where two chipmunks floated, no more than a foot apart from each other.

"Are they dead?"

"I think so." His face was pale. "You better get them out."

Just seeing those small, stiff shapes gave me goose bumps. "Dad—"

"Never make a coward's choice." He looked at me steadily. Then turned and went into the house.

My hands felt damp as I got a trash bag and the aluminum pole with the net. Slowly I dipped the net into the water, pulling it forward until it caught the body closest to me. Maybe I could get both at once. But when I lowered the pole, the chipmunk fell from the net. It sank slowly, turning over, then rose back to the surface. I squinted against the bright sun. The hot smell of chlorine clotted my nostrils. Pressing my teeth together, I bent for the pole, careful to try for only one of the chipmunks this time. After I'd caught it, I swung the net to the edge of the pool, but when I opened the trash bag to drop the small body into it, one of its stiffened claws was tangled in the net.

I wanted to run to my room. Stay there. But my father would only send me back out. And suddenly it didn't feel right anymore, obeying him, making the hardest choice. It was twisted around. Not the way it was supposed to be. Eyes blurry with tears, I searched for a twig to pry the chipmunk from the mesh. At first I was afraid of breaking its front leg, of hearing it snap, but after a while that no longer mattered. All I wanted was to get it over with. I threw the twig aside and, with my fingers, pried the rigid claw from the net. With a soft thud, the animal fell into the trash bag. Its eyes were black like crinkled leather. Getting the second chipmunk was easier. I left the pole by the water and carried the bag to the garage, where I dropped it into the trash can and pressed down on the lid. Only when I was soaping my hands and arms up to my elbows did I realize that my cheeks were aching and that I was still clenching my teeth.

I never told Eleanor about that day by the pool. Because I knew it would frighten her. Not just what my father did. But that I would obey like that. And the damage I was doing to myself.

Although we've been married four years now, I still follow the visiting pattern my parents drew up between them when they divorced—alternate Christmases. Thanksgivings belong to Eleanor's family. The first Christmas we were married we spent with my mother, who has a house just ten minutes from ours. She applied for a teaching job in Lincoln City soon after I moved there. Year two of our marriage, it was my father's turn to have us for Christmas. Like some gift he was entitled to. I didn't want to travel across Oregon to be miserable. Worried how he would be with Eleanor.

It was worse than anything I'd imagined. She admired the table he'd set with crystal goblets and the gold-rimmed plates he'd inherited from Austria. Told him, "You didn't have to do all that work for us."

My father slammed the oven door. "As you wish," he said, and removed the good china and silver and linen. Then he threw plastic utensils on the bare table and tossed paper plates as if they were Frisbees, making each one land between a plastic fork and knife.

"Quite a performance," Eleanor said calmly.

He squinted at her. "Let's sit down and eat."

"Good." To me, she whispered, "Can he control his temper?"

"I think he's showing off." I rolled my eyes, tried to pretend the whole thing wasn't as awful as it was.

Moonwalkers

The following day, he packed *Lebkuchen* and *Stollen* on two of the serving platters he'd yanked off the table just the night before, wrapped them into bath towels for us to take home, and when Eleanor objected, he persisted, "You can bring them back the next time you visit me."

In the hospital parking lot, a car door slams and a motor starts. Two motors. Probably visitors leaving.

I stand up. Against the slick linoleum floor, my shoes look scruffy. "I have a long drive back home," I explain. "I should—"

"You—" My father motions me close.

"Yes?"

"You—" His voice is hoarse, his breath shallow. He says something else I can't understand.

"Are you talking about Tiffany?" I shouldn't have mentioned her. Now he'll keep fretting about her and that poor Mrs. Lodge who is holding on to the forgotten child in school. Just as he frets about the librarian who bequeathed him her heart, and about her parents to whom she is lost. While he is carrying their daughter inside his chest as though it were a womb—the closest he has come to giving birth. His ultimate goal, I suspect. Though I've heard people say the human race would become extinct if men had to give birth, I believe my father would have gladly endured the pain of bringing forth children from his body. A dozen children. As many children as his body could yield.

"You . . ." My father's mouth is trying to shape itself around words.

I sit down again. Bend closer. "I'm sure Mrs. Lodge reached Tiffany's father that same day. He is probably a very good parent."

One of my father's pale hands makes a faint arch, as if to dismiss that possibility.

"This Mrs. Lodge," I say, "you know, if she—"

"You were conceived—"

"Let me fix your pillow," I offer quickly. I don't want to hear about my conception.

" . . . during the first . . . moonwalk."

Absurdly, I see my father and mother *coupling on the dimpled surface of a chalky moon, levitating parallel to each other in padded space suits, exposing only what is needed to conceive me.*

" . . . that summer of 1969," my father says. The bead of sweat between his eyebrows hasn't moved. Just sits there like a hardened drop of Crazy Glue. Some of his words slur as he tells me how my grandparents were visiting from Austria for an entire month that summer, staying with him and my mother in the green Victorian where they rented a small apartment on the second floor. To dodge my grandparents, my father would disappear with my mother into the bedroom and resume his attempts at having a new baby, to start his family once again, a large family, supplant my mother's sorrow for the girl she had miscarried. But for over a decade nothing had happened, though my father had begun to chart my mother's fertile days on graph paper. A *decade of fertile days.* And what he tells me about the moonwalk is that the television was on in the living room, right outside the bedroom, and that he and my mother could hear the voices of my grandparents marveling in German at the American astronauts.

As my father pauses, I'm left with the picture of my grandparents—long since dead—in the apartment where I grew up. *They have pulled the tufted sofa with its carved armrests up to the*

television. Behind them, a striped curtain hides a Sears refrigera-
tor-sink-stove combination and cupboards that will still smell of
nutmeg and scouring powder when I am a boy. Through the win-
dow I can see the peaks of the Wallowas. Across the hall lives a
man from India with pitted skin who works at the local shoe store
and wears black ties even on his day off. Though pets are banned
from the building, he has four cats; I'll never see them, but at
night I'll often hear them and learn to distinguish their cries.

At the moment, however, when my grandparents' trim bodies
lean forward, I have not yet been conceived. Their mountain-
brown faces are set in concentration as they witness the astro-
nauts take their initial steps across new territory.

"I think . . ." My father fidgets on his pillow. "I think they
felt lucky to be in America."

"Lucky?"

"They said it felt . . . nearer to the moon than Austria."

Lucky to have arrived here, to be with the son who left them
behind, the son whose German words are tinged by his American
life. I don't want to imagine my parents in the bedroom, *limbs*
entwined, their wishes giving shape to what is to become me.
What I want is to find out what is to become of my father now.
He seems quieter, kinder than he used to be. But what if it's not
the donor's heart that has done this? What if my father has been
like this all along, and I have failed to recognize him?

He's tugging at the neckline of his hospital gown, and I'm
stunned by the suddenness of my grief, know that this past
year—ever since he had his first heart attack—I have been
grieving for him. I just didn't know the language.

"I want to finish those books for her. I don't know how she
keeps track of all the different plots. . . . Bathrobes."

Somehow I figured I'd always be running from him. It's what I'm used to. What I'm good at.

"They sat in front of the television in those bathrobes. . . . Without knowing a word of English . . . went to the store and—" He frowns as if he's forgotten what he wants to say.

"Bathrobes," I prod him. "Television. Stores."

He nods. His voice becomes more coherent as he glides into memories that are nearly three decades old. How my grandparents read travel guides in German. How they navigated without the precise words to describe what they needed, relying instead on intuitive sounds and gestures. How pleased they were to be understood by the saleswoman who didn't speak one word of German and yet sold them those bathrobes. "The next day they went back to the store. She was . . . their first American friend, they said, and they brought her—"

Another gurney passes in the hallway. Then a man pushing a heavy floor-wax machine.

"—marzipan, John. Marzipan from Austria. Your favorite."

"My favorite. Yes. What color were they . . . those bathrobes?"

"Plaid."

"Plaid is not a color," I tease him.

"Plaid," he insists. Then adds, "Green and red."

I adjust the picture of my grandparents: *In their green-and-red-plaid bathrobes, they're leaning forward now, closer yet to the screen, as if, indeed, that will bring them nearer to the moon, and while they witness the astronauts' first uncertain steps, my father is keeping to what he's mapped out, traveling toward who I am to become, not embryo yet, not fused yet to my mother, only to my father's will as I drift toward him in the unknown, toward abrupt and brutal baptism in alien habitat.*

Moonwalkers

My father is silent in the alert way of great thinkers as he lies connected like a moonwalker to his life-support system, and as I sit by his bed, reaching through my discomfort and fear to assure myself he is here, *still here,* I lay one palm against his cheek, linking him to me. I feel him listening inward, trying to understand this female heart of his, while my grandparents *sit in front of the television, listening to foreign words as a white-padded figure bounces across the surface of an unfamiliar land-scape, while—in their own language, their own symbols—they too cross the chasm between what they hear and what they see.*

A Town Like Ours

Manfred and Kurt Rustemeier are twins who live in our parish. In a town as small as ours, twins are a rarity. We've only had one other set, the Friedman sisters, maiden ladies who both played the accordion and had to be relocated to Poland in 1941. That happened nine years after the Rustemeier twins were born. We celebrated the boys' christening at the Catholic church, witnessed their first *Kommunion*, watched them play soccer in the empty lots among the rubble of war, and we were not surprised when they married local girls on the same Sunday in May of 1952. They were twenty that spring, the Rustemeier brothers, too young to have fought in the war, too old to have grown up without the memories that none of us like to talk about and that we do our best to shield our children from. What we teach them is to value the good in their lives. To look ahead, not back. To be industrious. Pious. And above all, to obey. It is our way of going on. Regardless of what the world has to say about the *Vaterland*.

The first children of the twins were born within one month of each other, first Kurt's daughter, Helga, fair-skinned and wiry, then Manfred's son, Johannes, marked with the moonface of the sad and innocent. While Helga's movements were lively, the unfortunate boy turned his head sluggishly and regarded his surroundings through almond-shaped eyes. His damp lips would work themselves around sounds we couldn't understand. He was late to crawl, late to stand up and walk. At times we felt ashamed of the secret relief that *any* parent among us—whose child was not afflicted like Johannes—must have felt. It's because we've known the sorrow of having children like that taken from us. By the government or by God. How can anyone keep such a child safe?

Because we've seen how worries of that nature will tear at parents, we watched Manfred and his wife; but both Rustemeier families took care of the flawed boy and kept him alive. It didn't seem to matter to them to which parents he belonged, because the Rustemeiers often were together though they lived two blocks apart. What the boy liked to do was pull himself up by gripping the hem of a curtain, not hard enough to tear it down, but enough to steady himself, as if he understood the difference. He'd do this not only at home but also in our houses when the Rustemeiers visited, and it saddened us to watch his father and his Uncle Kurt with him, the immense patience—tenderness, even—of these tall men as they'd take the boy by the arms, trying to teach him to walk as if they believed they could make him whole, listening to his babbling as though real words were hidden somewhere in that singsong.

Like other young men who had not been seized from us by the war, the Rustemeier twins worked in construction, rebuilding the ruins of our town, while their wives sewed curtains, embroidered tablecloths, traded recipes and dress patterns, and kept their children clean. It was easier by then to feed our children. Only a few years earlier, we all had known what it was like to go to sleep aching with hunger, and then to wake to the sirens and bombs. Without coal, there were nights so cold we were sure we would freeze to death, as others had in our neighborhoods. We waited in long lines for scant rations, survived on thin soups boiled from *Kartoffelschalen*—potato peels—and *Rüben*—turnips. It was a time of upheaval, and we finally deserved order.

The year each Rustemeier wife gave birth to her fourth child, Manfred and Kurt inherited a meadow from their Aunt Hubertine, a meadow with cherry and apple trees, and with a swimming hole left by the Rhein centuries ago after one of its spring floods. Ever since they were small boys, the twins had played in that pond. A thin brook flowed through it, fanned out where it widened, and kept the water from getting too murky.

Behind the wooden shack, where their Aunt Hubertine used to store her canvas chairs and tools for her flower garden, stood a feeding trough where fat goldfish floated lazily. Years ago, the twins used to help her clean the trough. Now they taught their oldest children to care for the fish: first Helga would dart around the trough, catch their slippery bodies in a net, and set them into a washbasin; then Johannes, slow and methodical, would scoop out the scummy water with a pail. Together they'd scrub the sides and bottom of the trough and splash one another when they'd refill it with water from the pond.

Those two children were usually side by side, playing in the high grass, wearing crowns of daisies and cornflowers that Helga wove for both of them. She would tie Johannes's shoelaces when they came undone, remind him to wash his hands and face before eating. He adored it when she let him ride on back of her bicycle, his hefty arms around her middle, mouth wide to the sky in his nonsense chant, feet out at both sides because Helga had taught him to keep them away from the whirling spokes.

By the time all the Rustemeier children were in school—even Johannes, who was allowed to sit in the back of the classroom, where he dabbed spittle on his chalkboard with one thumb, painting damp and mysterious figures that vanished into the dull-gray slate as they dried—the twins had saved enough money to start building two houses. Many Sundays and weekday evenings the families worked on Aunt Hubertine's land, clearing and dividing it after much deliberation. To make certain their plots were equal, the twins measured them five times before they shook hands on the final allocation.

Hard workers, both of them, they set upon excavating and building the foundation walls from cinder blocks, helping one another by working on one house and then completing equal labor on the other, accomplishing far more together than they could have alone. And all along their wives brought food and assisted with some of the lighter work. The children would be playing by the rosebush that grew behind the trough, an immense bush with blossoms the size of cabbages, and we'd sometimes see the scarlet petals in their hair.

If the weather was warm enough, they'd swim in the pond. There, in the soft, greenish water, the moonfaced boy was more agile than his siblings and cousins. While on ground even the youngest children left him behind, Johannes glided and flipped through the water as though it were his natural element. Hot summer Sundays after mass, the twins and their wives would join their children in the water, and we'd hear laughter and singing from the pond. Often we'd come closer, on foot or by bicycle, to watch the contentment and prosperity of the twins with admiration and foreboding and the hope that maybe together the two families would be strong enough to thrive despite the sad-eyed boy.

As we'd look through the backyard of one of the houses, we'd notice the cinder-block walls of the other house growing, the same size, the same shape, and we'd watch the twins, their thick hair falling toward their eyebrows when they'd bend across the picnic their wives had prepared, or when they'd roll their *Zigaretten* after eating. In the evenings they'd pass our houses on the way home, the wives carrying bunches of roses that they'd arrange in painted vases and replace before the petals could stain their tablecloths.

It seemed to us then that the twins looked even more alike than before: both wore brown, squared-off beards and walked with the confident stride of men who take pride in ownership. The *Amerikaner*, who don't want to understand that we suffered too, have tried to teach us that any kind of pride is suspect in Deutschland; but it felt right to us when we saw that familiar pride in the twins, proof that it could never be totally squelched, and that—before long—pride would be there again, for all of us, in its purest form.

Among the qualities—aside from pride—that we value here are these: to pull pleasure out of the ordinary; to get along with one another. Because, surely, to get along and keep getting along with a reasonable degree of happiness is one of the greatest virtues. And when we looked at the Rustemeiers, who were more like one family than two, they seemed to have all that despite the burden of Johannes, and even more—they reminded us of who we really are, hardworking and high-principled people, who make the best of what we have, even if the world wants us to believe otherwise.

That's why it felt like a betrayal when—as the twins got ready to lay the joists for the second floors—the Rustemeier families stopped speaking to one another. In a town like ours, where most of us have been born and will die, and where our children and grandchildren will live and be buried, God willing, we know each other's stories and *Geheimnisse*—secrets. So we found out quickly that the feud had begun between the Rustemeier wives over something trivial—a rip in a skirt pattern. Manfred's wife, Brigitte, a feisty woman with long features and a reputation for making the smoothest gravies, claimed the rip was new, while Kurt's wife, Petra, who sang with the voice of an angel in the church choir but wore glasses so thick you could hardly see her eyes, insisted the rip had been there when she'd borrowed the pattern from Brigitte.

When this couldn't be resolved, the wives began to accuse one another of things they had compromised on before—like whose name had been listed first on the wreath they'd chosen together for Aunt Hubertine's funeral—and each wife declared the other was lying, until the husbands were drawn into their quarrel. Once they started, they both came to believe that they'd given in when dividing the land, that the other had gotten the better parcel.

Of course none of the Rustemeiers mentioned the boy, Johannes, in their arguments, though all of us felt confirmed in our worries that he was the cause of all this. Instead, the wives were bickering about who had married which brother. Brigitte—always one to take pleasure in giving to others—was convincing herself that she'd taken second best when she'd married Manfred; from there it escalated to Petra—known to be a peacemaker in town—believing that her sister-in-law had all along favored Kurt. There were questions. Suspicions. Manfred stopped talking to Kurt, figuring he must have encouraged Brigitte's affections.

After that, family gatherings simply became impossible. And yet the men still needed each other's help in building their houses. Of course they couldn't ask for it. A matter of honor. That fall, as they labored on setting the cinder-block walls of their second floors by themselves, their resentment seeped through our town, souring our dreams and spoiling fresh milk.

Though we didn't really believe a reconciliation was possible, we brought the Rustemeier families together at our weddings and christenings; we mentioned to one of the wives how much the other wife admired her flower beds, say, and we told the other how well her sister-in-law spoke of her *Graupensuppe*—barley soup—or *Herringsalat*; the priest visited both families after mass one Sunday, careful not to accept invitations to the midday meal from either in order to not offend the other; two of the nuns met with each wife in private and spoke of the heavenly rewards that forgiveness brings. But there is only so much any of us can say aloud, and then it is better to retreat to the good of the silence again.

Once summer arrived, it was regulated by written schedules, delivered through the *Briefträger*—postman—which family was permitted to swim in the pond at what times. The other Rustemeier children obeyed their parents' orders to stay away from their cousins, but Johannes would throw himself into the water he loved so much, howling when his father pulled him back. Despite repeated whippings with a wooden spoon—a discipline that has proven to be beneficial for most of our children—the boy didn't understand why he couldn't be in the pond while his cousins were swimming. Finally, his father erected a waist-high fence between the two buildings and extended the boards into the pond, where they jutted above the surface, slanting down until they dropped off after a few meters.

By tying a rope around Johannes's middle and fastening it to the cherry tree on his side of the fence, Manfred could let his son swim in his half of the pond; but Johannes, who was accustomed to doing most of his swimming under water, would butt into the fence and rise, a confused expression on his broad face. Whenever he'd attempt to scramble across the fence—because to stay away from his cousin Helga was unthinkable—his parents would shout at him from wherever they were working in the house, and he would flinch at their voices. Eventually Helga stayed away from the pond altogether. We'd find her watching Johannes from a distance, and the separation seemed as hard for her as for him. Sometimes she'd ride her bicycle alone, a pinched look around her mouth, as if she weren't eating enough.

Though the twins were diligent workers, the construction progressed as slowly as we predicted. It was as though, because their hearts were no longer connected, each of their bodies forgot what the other looked like. Both had always been large men with wide shoulders and wrists, but now there was a bulk to Kurt's body, a soft bulk that weakened him and hampered his movements. And when Manfred shaved his beard and mustache, it narrowed the shape of his face, emphasizing his chin, which had receded over the years.

We'd encounter the families in church, the twins on the men's side, pews apart, their wives on the women's side, each so aware if the other was wearing a new hat or new winter coat, and we'd bet that, soon, she too would be wearing something new.

Even the most tenacious among us were astonished by the twins' persistent complaints—always delivered by the *Briefträger*, of course: Manfred objected when Kurt planted his tomatoes early; Kurt wrote back that Manfred's family never watered the rosebush, which would have been dead long ago if he didn't care for it; Manfred was indignant when Kurt did not immediately repair the section of fence that had been damaged by a fallen tree on Kurt's side of the property. A total of eight letters were exchanged concerning the ownership of cherries that dropped from Manfred's tree onto Kurt's property.

It became unsettling to even see the twins from a distance. Because, to witness discontent, none of us has to go that far: it rages in our neighborhoods, inside our bedrooms. And what made it so hard to mediate was that the feud had been inevitable. Though its seed had lain dormant ever since the unfortunate boy's birth, it had ripened and finally burst through in that one trivial disagreement, negating all the accomplishments and celebrations the Rustemeier families had shared.

❧ ❧ ❧

A Town Like Ours

As the houses grew along with the children—Johannes faster than any of his siblings and cousins—the twins painted the stucco white and laid roof tiles that were made of red clay. But inside the houses were different: Manfred and Brigitte's woodwork was stained the color of honey, while Kurt and Petra's was chestnut-brown; Brigitte hung lace curtains and plants in her windows, while Petra preferred damask drapes; Brigitte covered her lamps with flowered fabric, while Petra bought simple white lampshades; Brigitte's wallpaper was striped, while Petra's had a border of intertwined leaves.

Just when it seemed that both families had grown accustomed to the distance that came with their feud, when someone would step from the front door, say, and not even furtively glance to note if anyone was outside the house next door, and when we too had woven that discontent into the cloth of our community along with the uneasy satisfaction that we'd been right all along, a sequence of events happened to change all that.

It began with a simple letter, something as insignificant as that skirt pattern—perhaps because it needed something equally small, a tool of sorts, to undo the tangle of so many misunderstandings. In this letter Manfred informed his twin brother that the fence obviously needed to be painted. To avoid buying clashing shades of green, he proposed he'd get enough paint for both sides, leave Kurt's share next to his mailbox, and have Kurt reimburse him by mail.

Five weeks after Manfred finished his side of the fence, we had one of those hot white July Sunday afternoons that take most of us out of our houses, waiting for a breeze to cool the air. Later, Kurt's wife would tell us that he took a nap after coming home from mass and eating three helpings of *Schmorfleisch und*

Kartoffeln—pot roast and potatoes—and that he woke up with his mouth dry. She knew this not only because the meat was a bit salty, but also because he emptied two glasses of water before he walked out to finally paint the rest of the fence.

While Kurt was blending the fresh green into Manfred's dried paint along the ridge, the moonfaced boy was playing on the other side with an armful of twigs. At thirteen, Johannes had reached his man-size, with a wide chest and solid legs and arms. Tied around his waist was the long rope that connected him safely to the cherry tree. Kneeling in the dirt, he crept backward as he arranged his twigs in one crooked line. Whenever he noticed another twig somewhere, he'd scuttle over on his knees, grasp it, and—mindless of the twigs he might drop in that effort—crawl back to his crooked line. From time to time he squinted into the sun, a pleased expression on his dirt-streaked face.

Despite the heat, Kurt was painting rapidly, but suddenly his brush caught between two slats and fell down on his brother's side. *"Verdammte Scheisse,"* he cursed. He hesitated. If he were to reach across the fence, he'd get paint on his clothes, and if he were to go around it, Manfred might accuse him of trespassing in yet another letter. Just then the boy stood up and ambled toward Kurt's brush, dragging his rope behind him. As he squatted to pick up the brush by the bristles, he managed to get more paint on himself than any of us would in a week of painting. Laughing aloud, he handed the brush to Kurt and reached up with both fists to wipe his eyes.

"No," Kurt warned, "you'll get paint in your eyes." He reached across the fence and held the boy's arms away from his face. "Don't move," he ordered. "You hear?" Heavily, he ran to the end of the fence, where we stood near the mailboxes, watching but not interfering as he looped back on his brother's side of the land. There he untied the rope from the boy's waist and led the boy down to the pond. "Hold still," he said, and made him sit on the grassy bank.

Johannes opened his mouth wide and splashed water at his uncle. Bending over the boy, Kurt washed the paint from his face and ears, from his sturdy neck and arms. Water ran down Kurt's shirt, down the boy's front, and the air was hot and moist with the scent of cut grass and roses.

Finally Kurt shook his head and laughed with the boy. "Look at the two of us," we heard him say. "Smeared with paint . . . and soaking wet. We may as well jump in." He untied the boy's shoes, then his own, and set them side by side.

We watched the two of them swimming in the center of the pond, beyond the confines of the fence. Kurt would dive, his long body leaving a cleft in the water as he'd submerge himself, and then the boy-man, Johannes, beaming and blowing water from his mouth, would stretch out his round arms and swim beneath his uncle. There they would lie, hover just beneath the surface like some antediluvian creatures, weightless, exuberant, studious. We'd wait for them to surface, and we'd suck air into our lungs to breathe for them.

Gradually, they would rise and then repeat their ritual, their stately bodies hanging one above the other, oddly sensual yet innocent, serious yet pleasureful. We saw their families step from their houses, Helga first, then Manfred, then the wives and the other children. Along opposite sides of the fence, they walked toward the pond, even Petra, whose voice usually carried farther than others. When Johannes and his Uncle Kurt emerged for air again, they didn't look surprised that they had an audience—it was, rather, that it didn't seem to matter to them as, once more, they heaved their large, graceful bodies beneath the surface, floating in a domain where feuds and intolerance—and even our concern—could no longer contaminate them.

The Juggler

My daughter loves a man who is turning blind. He is as tall as Zoe; yet, when he talks with her, he fastens his gaze to some place above her. His name is Michael, and he is the counselor at the elementary school where Zoe teaches. Though he can still see shapes, he can't make out details. Zoe has told me all this on the phone. She has also told me that, in another year, Michael won't even see shapes anymore.

The first weekend of October, she brings him across the Cascades to visit me in Coeur d'Alene. When she climbs from her car to embrace me, she looks radiant, face flushed, long hair tangled from driving with her window open. One hand on the small of her back, Michael enters my house as if leading her. He has the kind of profile I've seen on antique coins, and he moves like a dancer—a slow-motion version of a dancer—lithe and muscled and graceful.

After dinner, we drive to Spokane to see a movie, *Mona Lisa*. In front of the Magic Lantern Theater, a bearded man with a jester's hat is tossing one tricycle wheel and two flower-pots into the air. His pants are too big for him, and his tapestry vest covers part of his rumpled shirt. As the basin and swords come tumbling toward him, he laughs, hurls them back up, one long braid flapping across his back. The instant he drops the basin, I grasp Michael's shoulder, steer him and Zoe past the man, up the stairs of the theater.

Zoe settles him between us in the last row, and when the film starts, she translates the images on the screen for him. In the darkness, her whispered words form veils that obstruct the film. Where my elbow touches Michael's on the wooden armrest, it feels stiff. It's a stiffness that spreads: into my shoulders, my chest, my belly. Here I thought I had done all the letting go, had prepared myself for it since the day Zoe took her first uncertain step away from me, but it never occurred to me that I would turn her over to someone who'd need her this much.

She's whispering to Michael, and though I try to ignore her voice, I'm gradually drawn into its pulse, until it becomes part of the film. "Sshhh," someone hisses in the row behind us, but my daughter continues the rhythm of her interpretation.

I don't want the film to end.

In the late morning, Zoe and I pack the cooler for a canoe trip, and the three of us drive along the west shore of Lake Coeur d'Alene to the mouth of the St. Joe River. Led by my daughter's voice, Michael helps us lift the canoe from the roof rack and lower it into the water. While she paddles in front and I steer, he sits on a boat cushion in the belly of the canoe. Face raised toward the sun, one hand trailing in the water, he seems oblivious to the flashes of bottle-green light that filter through the layers of slow current.

The Juggler

"Are you still taking that carpentry workshop?" Zoe asks me.

"Wednesday evenings. Yes. I built two flower boxes."

"Great."

"Now I'm working on bookshelves."

"That's what I never have enough of—shelves."

"If these turn out all right, I'll build you some."

Dead trees jut into the river. Along the banks grow birches and oaks, and behind them are either clearings or denser stands of trees whose leaves haven't turned yet. I want to tell Michael how it will look here in two weeks, want to describe the reds and yellows I remember from other autumns, but I don't know how to offer something he hasn't asked of me.

When we pass three new cottages with huge windows facing the St. Joe, Zoe describes them to Michael. "Mom and I used to canoe here long before they were built. Behind them in the woods are railroad tracks, where we once found a pink freight train."

Michael tilts the side of his head toward me. His hair is curly, thick. "A pink train?"

I nod. And realize he can't see me. "Cotton-candy pink," I say.

"A hopper," Zoe adds. "It's been there for a long time. Mom and I climbed up the metal ladder in back and sat on top, eating peanuts. I wonder if it's still there." With her paddle she grazes a clump of reeds. "Mom, look. You can breathe through those reeds if you ever have to hide under water."

"Hollow reeds," I explain to Michael.

He laughs. "Thanks. I'll remember that the next time I want to hide under water."

Zoe turns, smiling at him with so much light in her eyes

that I have to look away. "You never know when you'll need it."

"As a kid, Zoe was very good at hiding." I switch the paddle to my left hand, pull it faster through the water. "So good that she wanted to be a detective."

"Cut it out, Mom." My daughter grins.

"Tell me more," Michael says.

"I became her main target. She spied on me brushing my hair, spied on me rehearsing for concerts."

"It's called surveillance, Mom. Besides—you gave me plenty of material. It was a year after the divorce, and you were just starting to date."

"Starting, yes, and thinking everyone but I knew the rules."

That year after her father left, Zoe baked almond cookies for me, convinced me to take ice-skating lessons with her, conspired with some of the musicians from the symphony to surprise me with a party on my thirtieth birthday. Sometimes I felt Zoe and I were growing up together. Other times I felt as though I were eleven and she thirty. She would stay up late to keep me company while I practiced the cello; often she'd fall asleep on the living-room sofa, fingers curved into her palm as if she were holding on to something.

"The one place I didn't follow Mom was the tree out back." Zoe leans back and, briefly, lets her head touch Michael's shoulder. "We have this tree, a cottonwood, white and huge. Mom would climb up there, sit for hours."

"It was a wonderful tree." I rest the paddle across my knees. "A comfortable tree. The neighbors never quite knew what to make of me sitting in the branches, but Zoe understood that I needed to be alone."

"My father's grandmother had thirteen kids," Michael says,

"and whenever she wanted to be alone, she brought up her apron and covered her head."

Zoe laughs. "She was probably wringing her hands."

"Sometimes," I tell Michael, who is turning toward my voice, "sometimes I woke up before my alarm went off in the morning, because Zoe was staring at me in her detective mode."

"You're lucky I switched career plans, Mom."

"Was that before or after you wanted to be an actress?" he asks her.

"Before. Actress was next. Then lawyer. Then actress again."

Michael and I both laugh. I like him—Or, rather, I could like him, if only he were not turning blind. Or if he were not with my daughter. I want more for Zoe.

The air feels crisp against our faces, the sun just strong enough to keep the chill from us. When a motorboat speeds past us, we rock sideways in its wake. We pass mudflats, cut through patches of scum formed by sawdust and spiderwebs. Ahead of us the right bank is covered with piles of logs that snag the river. Two small tugboats are tied to a dock.

I describe them to Michael. "Those tugs are used to push the logs to Coeur d'Alene and the lumberyards."

As Zoe tells him about the railroad tracks from the mountain and the trains that bring the logs down, she raises her hands and her words construct the railroad bridges that span the valleys between the hills.

All at once I want to know what it is like for Michael. Enveloped in my daughter's voice, I close my eyes and tilt my face toward the sky. Against my skin, the sun feels different: fuller; orange-warm. Beneath me, the canoe sways in the shallow waves that slap against its hull. Safe behind the backs of my daughter and her lover, I sit without sight, drawn into the pattern of their voices, into the sounds of the river, the rocking of the boat. A rail of shadows flits across my eyelids. Is this what Michael sees right now—that rapid sequence of bars? Or does everything appear to him in shades of gray?

"Would you like your jacket?" Zoe asks Michael.

"No. This is good. The way it is."

I squint. Trees divide the sphere of sun as it emerges and vanishes behind them.

We paddle for another half-hour before turning the canoe back. Waves catch us from the left as a motorboat passes, shift us toward the bank where a wooden rowboat, its green paint chipped, has been pulled into the marshy grass. Low and thin, the afternoon sun casts a slow path across the water as it takes on the sheen of pewter. A few streaks of light still flit across its surface, bounce off the tree stumps that rise from the river, their bottoms sodden, their tops bleached silver-gray. As we approach the lake, the water opens in front of us like a fan. For as long as I can, I follow the current with my eyes, reluctant to lose the river in the lake.

Michael takes a shower while Zoe and I sit in the breakfast nook, a bottle of red wine between us. It's the first time since her arrival that we've been alone, and suddenly I don't know what to say to her.

"Well?" She leans her elbows on the table, frames her face with her hands.

"He's bright and funny and very attractive. . . ."

"But?"

The Juggler

I know it would be better not to—still, I say it. "He won't always be like this."

A sudden bitterness darkens her eyes.

"I shouldn't have said that," I whisper. "I'm sorry."

She pushes her right thumbnail beneath her left, clicks them back and forth. We sit silently, until she blurts, "You remembered that train . . . the color . . . finding it."

"Yes . . ."

"You did not see it today."

"I don't understand."

"That train was still there for you today. Michael will remember things too."

"It's more than that, Zoe."

"If you knew him—"

"He'll need you. Far too much."

"That should feel familiar, then."

I see us skating on the frozen surface of the pond, see her sleeping on the sofa with her hands in fists, and feel the sum of my old needs spiral around me as if I were inside a child's spin-top.

"I'm sorry." My daughter's hand shoots out, alights on my wrist, cold and weightless, pulls me back.

I shake my head, keep shaking it.

But she keeps holding on to my wrist.

"I didn't know it was like that for you," I say.

Michael comes from the bathroom, his hair still damp. After that, I'm never alone with Zoe, and when they get ready to leave in the morning, her embrace feels flimsy, rushed. Long after her car has vanished, I stand in my driveway, waving. A lean wind moves through the purple mums in my flower boxes. The sun of late summer has stretched deceptively long into autumn, and the sudden shift feels like winter. In my arms, the tightness is back, and I rub them as I walk back into the house, where I listen to Vivaldi's *Echo* Concerto and brew a pot of ginseng tea that I forget to drink.

At noon, I drive to Spokane for a rehearsal. The concert is only three days away, and while we practice, I'm totally immersed in the music, but as soon as we finish, I'm back to worrying that I said all the wrong things to my daughter. I lock my cello inside my car, walk up the steps to the skywalks, a maze of glass tunnels that span the downtown streets between the second floors of stores. I buy a scarf for Zoe at The Bon, gloves for myself at Nordstrom's.

As I head back out to the skywalks, the clouds are darkening, and the only bursts of color come from the pavement below me, where the juggler is flinging about two swords and a tin washbasin. His baggy pants are tucked into yellow rain boots, and he's wearing his jester's hat again, each tassel a different color. While most people rush past him, a few stop. I stand transfixed, my palms against the glass wall. Whenever he drops something, he smiles and reaches down and juggles once again, pulling items from his mess of other stuff—always two of one kind and one of another: two bowling pegs and one picture frame; or two lampshades and one iron skillet—an uneven swirl without grace. And without fear. Fear of being ridiculed, for one. Of being wounded. If I could describe him to Michael, I would start with the lightness the juggler evokes in me, and I would tell Zoe that I want to believe in faith and risk and a world where you can stand beneath the gray October sky and flash your own colors through the air like a magician.

For Their Own Survival

That second winter without his wife, Sam Fulton returned to the Mexican village at the tip of the Baja, where rock formations continued to throw themselves into the ocean as if the land refused to end.

"I'll go crazy if you ever leave me," Liz had told him there on the beach next to the amber cliffs the day they had arrived. High above them in the bright-blue sky three vultures had floated as if attached to kite strings, their V-shaped wings without motion, waiting in this isolation with unending patience—beauty, even—as they tricked the hot white sun into their wings and snagged it in their feathers until they glowed blood-red.

"I love you so much, I'll go crazy if you ever leave me."

It wasn't the only time she'd made him promise he'd always be with her, but it was the time Sam kept coming back to whenever he tried to figure out why—after all her fears of losing him—she'd been the one to leave, after eleven years of marriage. The last thing they'd done together was the trip to Cabo San Lucas. It had been her idea to charter a fishing boat the day before they returned to Chicago, and when she hooked a marlin, the fishing pole left bruises on the insides of her thighs.

She would have lost the huge fish if he hadn't taken it for her and guided it through its last thrashings. In the water close to the boat, it looked iridescent and shining. It was different from any other fishing he'd done, far more exciting—like becoming a woman's first lover. When he'd met Liz, it had taken her so long to give in to him: she'd kept slowing him down, and he'd had to start all over again as if advancing in loops, though always a little further ahead and more certain of her.

As he hauled the marlin from the water, its color drained until it looked almost black. With the help of the mate, he tied the huge fish to the back of the boat, where it hung, dark and slack, its long spike harmless. That night he had their catch fried at the *palapa* restaurant across from the harbor, but Liz ate only the beans and rice and spoonfuls of fresh salsa. They drank margaritas until their lips burned from the coarse salt on the rims of their glasses, and when he made love to her on the mattress he'd carried out onto the terrace of their room, she kept her eyes shut. Her entire body tasted of salt. Her skin felt hot from the sun, and though he touched her cautiously, his fingers left long, white traces that vanished after he raised his hands from her.

The rest of the marlin he had frozen and shipped back to Chicago, but they never broiled the fillets with slices of lime and cilantro leaves as he'd planned. The wrapped packages were still in their freezer when Liz told him she wanted to live alone.

"I'll go crazy if I stay with you."

He held up one hand to block those words that, ironically, had reversed upon themselves. "Not like this—you can't say it like this."

For Their Own Survival

"I don't know," she said when he insisted on knowing why. "I don't know, Sam."

They used to do everything together: travel, hike, swim, take care of the garden and their two dogs. After they'd cooked gourmet dinners and gone for long walks, they'd often read aloud to one another—passages from biographies and travel journals—content in the house they'd designed and built on the side of a hill with a view of Lake Michigan. At times they congratulated themselves on their wise decision not to have children. "I'm glad we live in a time period," he would say, "where this is an accepted choice for women."

Without Liz, his days felt too open. During all the years of their marriage, she had never mentioned anything to brace him for her leaving. At first he thought of her almost constantly, anticipating her voice when he came home from work, expecting her sleep-warmed body next to him in the morning. Each time he had to remind himself that she was no longer there, it was as though he lost her all over again. The house felt unfamiliar, and he kept bumping into door frames and cabinets, misjudging distances.

Eating alone in the kitchen they had wallpapered together, he'd wonder what she was doing. He forced himself to wait for her return with confidence and declined dinner invitations from two teachers at the school where he was the principal. After work he shopped for food, mowed the lawn or cleaned the house, cooked a late meal, and walked the dogs until he was too tired to do anything but sleep.

From the library he borrowed books on the psychology of

women, trying to understand why Liz had left him. He found her type in most of the books: the woman who thought little of her abilities, who was afraid of success. When he'd first met her, she'd reminded him of the recruits he'd shaped in the late sixties, when he was a drill instructor for the army. During the few weeks in which he had them, he needed to break them down for their own survival—physically and mentally—taking away their essence before he could build them up as soldiers who would act identically in combat, who would trust the reflexes he'd instilled in them instead of relying on individual decisions. Not only were they equipped to kill, but they also knew how to die. Unquestioningly. He infused them with the kind of bravery that made them risk their lives for their buddies.

Though he didn't approve of the war, he did his best to prepare them for Vietnam. When it became too painful to send them off and read the lists of those who had been killed, he begged to be transferred to Vietnam, but he was so effective as a drill instructor that the army refused his request. Aching with the premonition of the recruits' deaths, he discovered their hidden cores, stripped them of their dignity, pushed their bodies beyond their limit of exertion. Very few of them understood that it was out of love when he took them down to where they were nothing, made them terrified of failing, and then rebuilt them. To do any less for them would have meant sending them off unprepared.

Liz had certainly been prepared when she had left him. She'd come into the marriage a shy, worried woman, a failed painter, and he'd scraped off her fears, her doubts, with infinite kindness and patience, until she no longer knew who she was. Only then, when she had become a blank canvas in his hands, could he draw a woman who was confident and poised, bold and successful. A few times he misjudged his timing, and she slipped from him.

"Stop pushing me," she'd cry. "Stop persuading me that I'm someone I know I'm not."

But gradually Liz came to embody this woman they both could be proud of. She returned to school, went to work for an advertising agency, and, the year before she moved out, opened her own firm. Sometimes, when she couldn't sleep late at night and asked him to hold her, she'd whisper to him of the wonderful changes he'd brought about in her, and they'd laugh fondly and reminisce about the woman he'd married as though she were a distant and embarrassing relative.

He spoke with Liz whenever she called, but he tried not to contact her, and it became easier because he could count on her need to talk with him at least once or twice a week. He'd agree to meet her for coffee at the Skylight Café, where they had often eaten brunch after a lazy Sunday morning in bed.

"I'm here for you," he would promise her. "Any time." He told her he wished she'd come home, but he followed the advice he found in the books: he never pressured her, and tried to ready himself for a life without her.

Though he determined it would be best for their marriage if he remained celibate, he went out to dinner with the science teacher, Sherrie Donalds, and invited his newly divorced neighbor, Ann Polk, to a concert. He bought a ticket to fly to New York for his college reunion, but the day before his departure, it struck him as absurd to travel anywhere until he had returned to Mexico and resolved what had happened there.

On his way to meet Liz for coffee, he traded in his New York ticket for a flight to Cabo San Lucas. She sat waiting for him at a table next to the salad bar, where a nativity scene had been set up below the plastic sneeze-guard—gaudy plaster figures surrounded by miniature churches with flickering lights. Someone had sprayed snowflakes on the sneeze guard and placed poinsettia plants at either end of the salad bar. Strings of red bulbs decorated the skylights and made Liz's hair look pink, synthetic.

"Call me," she said, "when you get back from your reunion."

He didn't tell her he was flying to Mexico instead. Exhilarated and afraid that she wouldn't know where he would be, he sat across from her, close enough to touch.

He stayed at the last hotel on the Pacific side of the Baja, a low sequence of white buildings that respected the stark beauty of the land. The cats were still there, dozens of them, the color of the cliffs, dozing in the sand beneath the bushes, invisible until they stirred or darted away. Waves came in high and crashed down like shelves overcrowded with books—abrupt and massive.

Though he wasn't able to get the room he'd had with Liz two years earlier, his was identical, with wrought-iron chairs, a woven bedspread, three wood-framed mirrors, and a terrace that faced the ocean. Red-tiled paths bled into his room—cool and smooth beneath his bare feet. In the narrow gap between the back of the hotel and the cliffs lay a garden of hibiscus bushes, palm trees, and cacti.

For Their Own Survival

After he unpacked, he hiked south along the Pacific beach toward the two rock formations that stood between him and Playa de Amor, lovers' beach, the only strip of sand open to both the Pacific and the Sea of Cortés, where he and Liz had snorkeled. A boat from the harbor had dropped them off one morning and picked them up at four, several hours later than expected. When the sun became unbearable, they'd retreated into a cave formed by huge yellow boulders that made them feel as though they were inside a cathedral.

This time he would approach the lovers' beach on foot, arriving and leaving when he chose to. But when he reached the cliffs, they seemed impossible to cross. He discovered a scant trail of sand grains where people had climbed before him, and he used each crevice for leverage to push himself off. As he stood on the ridge where the tip of the peninsula met the ocean and the bay, swift winds stroked the surface of the water. He used to like this definite sense of geography, knowing exactly where he was in relationship to the rest of the earth. He had felt that certainty in his marriage too—being able to point to where he was—but now that had vanished, and this mass of land no longer felt secure to him either. A huge wave could wash over it at any moment, erode the sands and cliffs, the hotel.

He kept having dreams of his house sliding down the hill and folding upon itself at the bottom of the driveway. One night he dreamed of it filled with gaudy flames that unfurled like paper poppies; another night his assistant principal, who was far too lenient with the students, broke into his house and gave a party for the teachers and administrators. He'd wake up disoriented, depleted by sleep instead of restored, as if the place had chafed away at him during the night. Papaya juice would burn his throat, and the sun would make his eyes ache.

He bought sunglasses and a straw hat. Sometimes he talked to the old woman from Germany who had the room where he'd stayed with Liz. She'd sit in the sand for many hours, watching the waves, her gray hair loose on her shoulders. Her name was Frau Dönstetter, and the waiter who silently poured his coffee from an arm length's distance—dignified and focused, as if he were performing surgery—liked to laugh and talk with the old woman when she ate her meals on the restaurant patio, feeding scraps to the cats that were all around her, swift shadows of the sand.

Early one morning Sam walked to the harbor and tried to locate the boat he'd chartered with Liz. When he couldn't find it, he settled on a smaller fishing craft and rode the calm waters of the bay past Playa de Amor and around the arch into the churning Pacific. The boat passed the beach where his hotel stood, its contours low and rounded like boulders worn smooth by the waters, and headed parallel to the shore toward the old lighthouse—*el faro viejo*. He caught only sailfish, bonitos, and cabrillas, and told the captain to keep the catch. That evening he walked the long, empty beach from his hotel to the northern outcropping of rocks, where a crumbling set of stone steps led up to the town that curved itself around the harbor and spilled across the hill until it was blocked by the Sea of Cortés.

In one of the bars he sat with a bottle of *cerveza* in front of him, a man alone—an oddity in this town that was crowded by men in groups of three or four who'd come from Europe and America to the end of the Baja for some of the best marlin-fishing in the world. They abandoned the town early in the mornings on chartered boats, but at night, in the bars, they traded fishing stories and invented their lives. "I'm in the film industry," one man announced, keeping it vague whether he was a clerk or a producer. Another man bragged about renting a house on the Pedregal, the wealthy part of town, where tile-roofed villas clung to the stone cliffs like garnets. Sam drank quietly, and he pitied the men as they tried to impress one another: size of fish, size of boat, size of house.

In the morning he recognized the boat and captain from two years before. And on the other side of the stone arch he found his marlin as though it had summoned him. It charged out, paused, then changed its direction. He let it resist him, let it hurl itself from the water and strain against the line in its tremendous urge to stay alive. He felt the marlin's will, separate from his. Whenever it halted its struggle, Sam regained the line and lured it closer. To keep it from eluding him, he had to tire it, let it play its game, wait it out without exhausting himself.

As he brought it against the boat, its stripes—bluish and black, iridescent—had already dulled. Gulls and cormorants circled the boat—vultures of the sea—and the mate stepped next to him, ready to gaff the marlin. Already Sam could see its massive body fastened to the back of the boat, could feel its cold skin with the flaky scales—coarse if he were to stroke his hand toward its spike, smooth if he were to rub his hand toward the tail—and all at once he wanted to release the fish before the color drained from it completely, watch it shimmer as it disappeared along the boat, think about it when he was back home, and know it still belonged to him in the depth of the Pacific.

"Wait." He caught the mate's arm and bent across the side to twist out the hook, but as the marlin turned dark and reached its point of nothingness, he could not abstain from pressing his hands against the taut skin as if to infuse the great fish with his spirit. For a moment, there, it felt as though the scales were coming off in his palms, leaving the outlines of his hands on the marlin, and as he let it go, it darted away, heaving itself into life—forever altered, its colors more radiant than before.

Lower Crossing

This June, the Spokane River is running higher than I've ever seen it, spilling in white torrents across the volcanic rocks, dragging trees into its current. The wishbone shapes of their branches trap the river in silver arrows, then release it, yield. Already, two people have drowned: a car mechanic who dived from the footbridge between the Jesuit college and the yuppie condos, and a student from Lewis and Clark who tied a rope between herself and her inflatable raft because she didn't like life preservers.

The fitfulness of the river resonates throughout Spokane. When I take my old dog, Basil, for his walk early this morning, pools of shards glitter in the sun outside the gay bar on the corner of Monroe.

"Watch out." I pull Basil away from the shattered glass. It has happened here before—some rednecks heaving bricks into the parked cars at night—and it pisses me off, makes me want to smash their windows too. "Damn rednecks," I tell Basil.

He sways, and I press my palms against his yellow flanks, keep them there, murmur to him while he steadies himself.

129

"You know what we should do, you and I? Hold vigil here some night. Sit on the curb and wait for those rednecks. And if they ask if we're here to make sure the perverts can dance, I'll tell them that you and I are here to scare perverts like *them* away. All you have to do is growl at them. And look ferocious."

As a young dog, Basil used to race toward me like a bullet— sleek and powerful, looking ferocious—yet always stopping himself inches before he could knock me over. So polite. But strangers were frightened when he came at them like that, because they had no idea how gentle he was.

"Damn rednecks."

Throughout Basil's body, I can feel how anxious he is about falling, as anxious as he has been lately about getting up. Often, his legs will splay outward, landing him flat on his belly like a seal. And here I am recruiting him in my attack-dog fantasies. He's the kind of dog who doesn't like looking foolish. That's why he'll hesitate before easing himself down the steps into our yard, before climbing into my sister Ev's station wagon. Dignity is essential to Basil. Dignity and politeness. First thing every day he waits for me by the fridge, nudging me to dip my finger into his fudge jar and coat half an aspirin for him. He'll lick my finger, my hand, lick hard and swallow. Without the fudge, he would spit out his medicine in a second. Whenever I wash his saliva from my hands, I feel sad for Basil. Sad for all I haven't done for him. And fucking scared. For myself. Because he can't last much longer.

"Hey, we're almost there," I tell him.

He shakes himself almost playfully, tries to run, to pull me along. *Bad choice*. Moments like this, when he forgets his aches and gets exuberant, I can still recognize the puppy in him. He'll hear the crinkling of cellophane coming off a new rawhide bone, say, or watch me tie my Nikes, and he'll try to leap up and down. Inevitably, though, he'll get that puzzled expression on his face, because his body will remind him that he is an old dog.

As it does now. Bringing him to a stop. His chest is heaving, pumping, and when he moves forward along the sidewalk and across the street with me, it's on legs that are stiff, so stiff. Twelve years ago, when Ev and I first saw him at the Spokanimal shelter, he was playing in a kennel with another gorgeous yellow pup, his brother, the two of them a sun-colored tangle of legs and tails until his brother spotted us and scurried across Basil to court us with yelps and with licks, showing off by standing on his hind legs and rolling on his back, reminding me of those popular kids way back in school who'd always seemed so sure they'd get picked first. Basil, however, made no effort to win us over, and when I told Ev he was the one I wanted to adopt and why, she smiled and nodded, because she had never been one of the popular kids either. And all along, Basil sat there quietly, one ear cocked, observing us with the dignity of a much older dog.

The dog he now has grown into.

At the Street Café, I slip the end of his leash around the iron leg of an outdoor table, as usual. "I'll be right back with some water for you," I promise, but when I return with my coffee and his water, he's no longer there. I set both paper cups on the table, step into the road, whistle. "Basil . . . Basil?"

While I'm checking the rear parking lot, Moss, who works at the Street Café, sticks her head from the kitchen door. "Basilboy . . ." she chants, breath warm with milk and granola. Her black hair is spiked, showing its blond roots. "Hey, Basilboy . . ."

Moss's real name used to be Lucy. Lucy Ferdinand. That was before she left her family and went to divinity school at Yale, where she lasted seventeen months. Now Moss believes she is meant to meditate and cook in the Pacific Northwest. Her specialty is a tangy garbanzo stew with tons of curry and specks of unidentifiable green. When she serves your food, she stands so close you swear she's in lust with you. It makes some customers real jumpy; but after you've been around her enough, you can see that she stands this close to everyone, women and men. If you step away, she only follows.

"I'll help you look." The screen door slams behind her.

"He can't have gotten far," I tell her as we cross the Monroe Street Bridge to downtown. "You know how slow he is with his arthritis."

Usually I stop halfway across this bridge: it's the best spot to watch the rapids—on one side the lower falls, on the other the downriver gorge—where they plummet one hundred fifty feet in the center of Spokane. They're almost entirely white—that's how fast they are—coating my face with their cool breath as wind tunnels beneath them. For me, waterfalls are mesmerizing the way fires are, making it hard to look away. But today, I rush through their mist. On the other side of the bridge, two cars and a truck with a gun rack are waiting at a stop light.

"Basil." I whistle. "Come here, good boy. . . ." But the only one I see is Moss, leaping into my field of vision wherever I turn to search.

"Basil still has life in his eyes," she tells me.

"He is old. And not very strong."

When Basil was younger, I used to walk him on the river trail that starts at the falls and ends near the old Shriners Hospital. Halfway in between is our neighborhood, a handful of houses that sit high above the north bank, hidden by lush vegetation. Here, the bed of the river is wider than downtown, more lake than stream, the shape of a snake that swallowed a sheep. Though we live just a mile downstream from the falls and the stores, most people don't realize our neighborhood exists. It's so secluded that we might as well be hours away from the city. And we rather like that.

This past year, the river trail has become too uneven for Basil, and he can no longer negotiate the steep path between the trail and our house. When Ev and I were girls, we used to clear that path every May with our father, who was as impatient as we to swim, though the water was still cool; but now we merely whack at the dense weeds and shrubs and sumacs every few years to keep them from absorbing our path altogether into the overgrown hillside that turns amber and dry before the end of summer.

"You think Basil is afraid?" Moss asks.

"Of porcupines. He went in for porcupine quills and—"

"You've told me the porcupine story, Libby."

"He is also afraid of water. You've seen him—he'll go right up to the edge, but never in, and when Ev and I swim, he just runs along the bank, yelping as if he wanted to rescue us."

"What I meant was . . ." Moss presses two fingers against her high forehead and circles them. Her face is all forehead, her hair short like a boy's. She's the only blonde I know who darkens her hair deliberately, and she snips at it every day the way some men snip at their beards.

"What I meant was," Moss says, "afraid of dying."

"Not nearly as afraid as I am of him dying."

133

"You'll know it's time for him to go when the life in his eyes goes dim."

Moss said the same thing last Sunday to Ev and me when she served us eggplant kabobs. Life is one of Moss's passionate subjects: it's something she "embraces" and "balances." Ev and I see her at least once a week when we eat at the Street Café. Our regular table is next to the chocolate carousel, the cake display where a dozen variations of chocolate cake revolve behind curved glass. Food at the Street Café never tastes the same twice in a row. That's what Ev and I like about it. That's why we endure the long wait that, inevitably, is part of eating here. Moss is an inspired cook, the only one who's worked at the café for longer than a year and who seems to follow some kind of schedule. At least most days. Employees here change frequently, bringing with them flowing garments and hair, traipsing between the stoves and dining tables in their Teva sandals or combat boots, tinkering with recipes they remember from a grandmother or have unearthed in ethnic vegetarian cookbooks published by communes that dissolved decades ago.

"My boyfriend, he gave me a black rose the other night," Moss tells me as we walk past the construction site of the new library.

"The kind of red that's almost black?"

"No. Totally black."

"Basil . . . Basil . . ." I check the street next to the library. Nothing. I'm so impatient for this library to be completed. Our temporary library has been squeezed into what used to be J. C. Penney, and it has to share the building with a discount store that, I swear, employs more detectives than salespeople. You can never locate what you came in for, but there's usually a man in a cheap suit stalking you. And that's damn distracting. And tempting. Tempting because it makes you want to test how good those detectives really are and, even though you've never thought of shoplifting, to snatch a pair of ninety-nine-cent socks, say, and a three-dollar tie and stuff them into your pockets. The only decent thing we ever bought there was a purple terry-cloth robe for Ev. We avoid shopping there, because we don't particularly enjoy feeling like suspects. Besides, the store has a lousy return policy—store credit only—which means you have to endure another one of those lovely shopping experiences. *No, thank you.*

"My boyfriend says they're supposed to last longer."

"What?"

"Black roses."

"Make sure to drop a penny into the vase."

We take the Lincoln Street Bridge back across the river. In the fenced playground of the YMCA, the day-care toddlers are playing, diapers pressing their squat legs into O-shapes. One pale, stocky girl is reaching through the metal links with a plastic shovel to get the dirt on the outside of the fence. I can imagine what my sister would make of that. *"That girl will always be like that,"* she'd say, *"wanting what's outside her own boundaries. Like you, Libby."*

Please. I used to think boundaries were the lines between countries, but Ev has been talking a lot about what she calls personal boundaries. Her own boundaries. Her professor's boundaries. Our neighbor Gloria's boundaries. Our paperboy's boundaries. Moss's boundaries. Lately even the river's boundaries as it pulls lives into its current, growing fat on souls.

These days, Ev is into textbook interpretations. After twenty-four years of working with me in the plant shop that our parents started, Ev is now taking psychology classes and telling me that my boundaries are inconsistent. She never mentioned returning to college—not until she started on speed. Legal speed: methylphenidate. Her doctor wrote a prescription for her when she complained about getting drowsy while doing our accounts. Within a week of swallowing speed, Ev built a wooden bicycle-rack, hosed down the walls of our potting shed, designed a stained-glass window in six shades of green for the plant shop, brought home college catalogues, registered for classes, and started dating a student half her age, a chaste and brainy encounter, I suspect, like most of Ev's encounters. She thrives on passion of the mind, prefers it to the messiness of bodily passions.

I know all the reasons why it's foolish to live with my sister when, together, we're a century old. Ev's fifty-one, I'm forty-nine, and we've never been apart. Including the year when I was nineteen and married to Billy Wood, who moved in with me and my parents and Ev. Maybe that's why Billy and I didn't make it to our first anniversary. One Sunday we broke up in Knight's Diner after ordering breakfast. We were arguing, loudly, as we often did the instant we were out of the house, and just as our favorite waitress, Marie, was bringing our plates, Billy shoved his chair aside and stomped out. Since I didn't want to be rude to Marie, I ate my eggs over easy, certain that everyone in Knight's Diner was staring at me while I sat across from Billy's waffles.

Marie touched my hair. "Libby . . . You want me to take those away, Libby?"

"No . . . I'm really hungry today."

Lower Crossing

Whenever I go over things I would do differently in my life, I'm sure I would not sit by myself at that table in Knight's Diner, swallowing eggs over easy I no longer want while pretending nothing is wrong, and then swallowing Billy's cold, spongy waffles that—on bad days, I swear—I can still feel sitting on the bottom of my stomach. Greasy. Queasy. Instead, I picture myself raising one hand and signaling Marie for the check, paying it calmly. Or, better yet, without bothering to ask her for the check, dropping a twenty on the table, more than plenty for two breakfasts and a large tip.

Seeing myself like that is enough to make me want to go through that breakup again, to get it right this time. Except I wouldn't want to sit across from Billy Wood again. Not even to give myself that satisfaction. Besides, a breakup would presume a relationship. And there hasn't been anyone else since. Not really. Unless you count the times I cruise the home-improvement stores to pick out a two-day-fellow for myself. One day for the get-acquainted-fuck, one day for the goodbye-fuck. It's that basic.

Moss raises her face, sniffs the air. "Yeast," she says.

I inhale deeply, draw in the warm, thick smell of the Wonder Bread factory, a smell that hugs the north bank of the river. While I love that smell, Ev claims it puts weight on her. She frets about her size even though she's barely an eight.

"Basil." I glance over my shoulder, and Moss's entire body follows that motion. "Stop hopping around. Please?"

"Sure, Libby." But she can't keep still.

"Sorry for snapping at you."

"Have you ever sold one?"

"Sold what?"

"A totally black rose."

"Not totally black."

"I thought maybe my boyfriend got it from your shop." She frowns. "Anyhow, that Christmas cactus you gave me last year . . . it's getting spots."

"What size are they? What color?"

"Tiny. And white. It's getting crusty too."

"What do you mean by crusty?"

"An inch or two where it comes out of the earth . . . it's sort of hard and dry there."

"Why don't you drop it by the shop? I'll see what I can do for it."

From behind a stack of bald tires, a brown dog snarls at us, lips puckered from its teeth.

"Don't," I warn Moss as she hunkers down.

But she's already extending one hand toward the dog.

"Wrong dog," I tell her. "Ours is yellow."

Just then, the dog darts forward, tail clamped between its legs.

"Moss—"

"Don't be so frightened." Her eyes are enormous.

I have no idea if she's talking to herself or to me or to the dog who, amazingly now, is nuzzling the wristband of her watch. "Let's go, Moss."

She starts massaging the dog's throat. Proceeding to his pink belly as if settling in for a while with him. "I learned that at a retreat in Ritzville last weekend," she tells me without looking up. "Actually, it was a retreat for horses and for people. We slept

138

nude under the stars. And in the morning we massaged the horses."

I'm right back in junior high, trying not to giggle as Frankie Marinelli whispers to me that Catherine the Great used to do it with horses. "She had herself strapped underneath the horse. Right underneath, in a leather sling. Get it, Libby? Because men's boners weren't big enough to fill her up inside."

Moss sighs. "It was magical. . . ."

I fight the image of Moss strapped beneath some horse Catherine-style. "Basil," I shout, and start walking away from her. "Basil?" I whistle. "Come here, good boy. . . ."

But she's following me, hopping in front of me. "Those horses transformed under our hands, Libby. . . . All their tension and aches floated out of them and into our hands, vanished . . . and then we rode them. They were so . . . balanced, the horses, Libby, extensions of us, of our own harmony. Normally I'm sore after riding."

"So was Catherine."

"Who?"

"Catherine the Great."

"Except she copulated with the horses," Moss says calmly.

I stare at her. Feel my face go hot.

"But everyone knows that, Libby."

As I check the alley between the Street Café and the barber shop for Basil, I can already see myself telling Ev about Moss and those horses. She likes to insist Moss was hatched on some other planet. "A different way of being in the world, Libby. Like from far, far away and without a clue."

139

Last month we somehow ended up taking Moss to the Civic Theater with us, though we had no plans to do so. We were eating dinner at the Street Café, talking about the new Harnetiaux play we were about to see, when Moss pulled a chair to our table and asked if she could come to the theater with us. That's how she is—she says what she wants the instant she thinks of it—and I have to admire that. Even though it sometimes bugs me.

Ev stalled. She took off her bottle-thick glasses, cleaned them on her scarf, and pretended to glance around the café though—without glasses—she's practically blind.

"It's rather crowded here tonight," I said. Aside from Moss, only the blond boy cook with the Whoopie Goldberg braids and the pierced eyebrows was serving food.

"It may not be fair to the other customers to take you away," Ev suggested.

"They don't mind waiting."

"You may not be able to get a ticket."

"Then I'll come back here," Moss said, and got her woven cape from the kitchen.

In the basement theater, she wedged herself between Ev and me, lean elbows hogging both armrests. Where most people will make room for your arm if you touch them accidentally, Moss presses closer. "*You two*," she said, "have the absolutely best sister-relationship I've ever come across."

"You have a tendency," Ev said, "to romanticize what we have."

"I don't have anyone who looks like me. With *you two*, it's obvious that you are sisters. You're lucky."

I glanced at my sister. We both have small chins and wavy hair. But Ev definitely looks a lot older than I. Of course I would never tell her that. While my hair is more brown than gray, hers is almost entirely gray, and that's more obvious now that she's a student and letting it grow.

"We have lots of differences too," I said. "Ev always has cold feet, while I go sockless into winter."

"Yes, and Libby leaves shoes all over the floor, while I pick mine up."

"But *you two* talk to each other." *You two.* Moss said it with awe.

"Well . . . yes," I said. "We do that. A whole lot of that."

"Occasionally too much," my sister added.

When Moss and I can't find Basil, we go inside the Street Café and call Spokanimal. But just as I'm reporting my dog missing, Moss points to the door. Behind its milky glass, the silhouette of a broad-bellied man slides past, tilted back as if tied to something he's dragging along. Instantly, I'm by the door, and there's the barber from next door, attached to my dog and my dog's leash.

"You found Basil," I yell.

"I took him for a nice walk."

"You did what?"

"He was whimpering. So I untied him from the table and—"

"I wish you hadn't done that." I say it softly, very softly, to keep from screaming. But then I remember Knight's Diner and Billy Wood's spongy waffles. And I do it right. "Don't you ever do that again," I scream at the barber.

He flinches. Drops the leash. Raises both hands as if I were pointing a gun at him. "No reason to make a fuss."

I feel his powerlessness at being accosted by me. Feel it as strongly as my fear of losing Basil altogether. Soon. But not yet. "Bang." I aim my right forefinger at the barber's heart. Cock my thumb. "Bang. Bang."

His eyes skim across me, then Moss, as if we were one of a kind, not quite fit for a neighborhood in Spokane—not his neighborhood, anyhow—and walks off in his pointed cowboy boots.

"All right?" I crouch, stroke my dog's long, yellow jaw. "All right now?"

"Basilboy," Moss croons. "Such a handsome dog you are."

As I lean my face against the top of Basil's head, I feel the bony ridge that runs up the length of his nose and between his eyes and ears. His fur smells of dust and sun the way a hayloft will in the afternoon, making you sneeze. It's the same smell he had the day Ev and I first brought him home, a smell that, however, didn't last for more than an hour, because he scrambled through our yard and down the steep hillside to the river trail, where he managed to get himself skunked. After we bathed him in eight gallons of cheap tomato juice, he smelled like spaghetti sauce about to spoil, and the children in Lower Crossing stopped petting him, because the residue kept coming off his fur for days.

Lower Crossing is the name of our neighborhood, because— according to Gloria Müller next door—the Spokane Indians used to cross here late every summer. Gloria does it too. Although she's not from the Spokane tribe but half Scottish and half German. Every August—even now, at eighty-four—Gloria waits for that day when the river recedes far enough so that she can walk across the huge stones in the riverbed as if they were evenly spaced railroad ties. She balances her tall body by extending her arms, and when she reaches the other side, she sits beneath the enormous cottonwood tree, her back against its trunk, her face turned to its leaves. I know because these last few years I've crossed with Gloria, though she insists she doesn't need help.

"You're the one helping me," I tell her. "I want to be with someone who's done this before."

"Stop bullshitting me, Libby. You are a swimmer—not a convincing liar."

"It's not that. It's because I have this fear of the entire Spokane River coming at me all at once in one giant red—"

"Red Sea? Your father read too many Bible stories to you when you were a child."

"Probably. I think he read them to himself. I just listened."

"Stories . . ." Gloria snorts. "And not even good ones."

Gloria is a fierce atheist who has lived in Lower Crossing since she was a child. For me, she has always been old—a woman older than my parents when I was born; in her eighties now that I'm approaching half a century. When her grandson, Jesse, visits her on weekends, he races up the steps of our front porch, eager to play with Basil. He would like to teach Basil to swim in the river with him, but our dog is skittish near water. He'll get his paws wet, but that's about all, and he gets agitated when any of us swim. My sister doesn't much like to have Jesse around—she says he lies—but I love listening to him tell me about the two bears that live inside the hedge at his preschool; about the apples on his grandmother's trees; about stars talking to him through his glass roof; about how he saw Basil in the dentist's chair when his father had a swollen tooth. . . .

Jesse is still too young to separate his inner and outer truths, and whenever I'm near him, I feel as though I, too, live in that gap of light where everything is equally real. It's one of the few times when I regret not having a child of my own. Usually I don't let myself go there in my imagination. It's too risky. Because I'm capable of imagining almost anything. With Billy I made the imagining of our marriage stronger than the marriage. I can do that with almost anything.

My sister says that I'm drawn to people like me who are on the fringe. Like Moss and Gloria and Jesse. I'm flattered. Because I wish I could live even closer to that fringe, wish I could always see the world the way Jesse does.

Whenever Ev corrects him—clarifying what she considers real, and what she considers a lie—Jesse frowns at her as though she were telling him lies. And already he'll be turning to me, describing his latest discovery, the most recent a frog with three tongues.

"And then what happened?" I ask him.

And then . . . It's what moves Jesse forward. Always.

Into yet another fabulous truth. "And then the frog—a red frog, Libby—"

"Yes?"

"—it jumped out of my cereal bowl and then my Grandma Gloria caught a lion and made a drum from his head and then—"

"Not lions," Ev interrupts.

"Yes so. Lions and alligators and rhinoceroses," he insists.

Many of Jesse's stories have to do with the drums his grandmother builds from pottery and animal hides. He is fascinated by those drums. When Gloria plays them, she sits with her sturdy legs crossed and leans toward the drum as if driving a motorcycle. She has shown Jesse and me how to start the beat from our palms and let it spread into our arms till we can feel it in our chest, our legs, and down into the earth. Gloria has been drumming long before drumming became fashionable for the men's groups that flock to the forests north of Colville, where the locals are suspicious of fellows who have encounters in the woods with fellows for purposes other than logging, getting shit-faced, or shooting Bambi.

Though Gloria feels mildly embarrassed for those white fellows with their drums and their vision quests and their sweat lodges and fire pits, she provides them with drumming lessons and made-to-order drums, using the booty—as she says—to revamp her house: a Jacuzzi; three skylights for Jesse's room; a screened porch.

All through July, the Spokane continues to run mud-colored and high. A teacher from Cheney drowns when his borrowed canoe is overturned by a drifting log. But gradually, as the river dwindles, it loses its force. From our kitchen window I can make out the shapes of some boulders beneath its surface. They're not big enough to redirect the water; yet, they sculpt its flow. Come August, they will emerge fully, as they do late every summer, scaly and gray-white, waiting for an occasional swell to wash across them and let them glisten for a brief while. Waiting.

Waiting. As Gloria is waiting to cross over. As Ev and I are waiting. We want these last months with Basil to move slowly. Like clumsy magicians, we pull bliss from our pockets of sadness. He tolerates our bungled efforts to distract him from his pain, praises us with a listless wagging of his tail.

One night a bat gets into the shower with Ev, who has no

idea what it is because she's not wearing her glasses, only feels that something is there. When she starts cursing and crying, I rush into the bathroom, yank Ev's purple bathrobe from the hook next to my sweats, and trap the bat inside the robe. I shake it out under the stars, and there's Basil, right next to me, then Ev, who has pulled on her blue-rimmed glasses and my old sweats.

"Why did you have to use my bathrobe?" she wants to know.

"Forgive me. If it happens again, I'll leave you screaming."

"I didn't mean it like that."

"You're welcome."

"Thank you, Libby. Will that do?"

"If you make my bed for a week."

She laughs. "Dreamer."

On the grass ledge high above the river, she spreads her purple robe, and we sit on thick terry cloth, our arms around Basil. We tell him stories of when he was a young dog. Basil stories: stories about how he wasn't interested in learning to fetch but made up much smarter games instead—a crazy dance, and his own version of hide and seek; how polite he was by nature, not all over you like most puppies, but waiting for you to touch him first. . . .

The air smells like Wonder Bread, and the stars are so sharp and so white that it feels as though we were in a lunar landscape. *A lunar landscape that smells like Wonder Bread.* I laugh, and when I feel Ev looking at me, it's one of those moments when I know that this here—with my sister and my dog by my river—is where I am content to be. Now. And I think how right Moss is whenever she talks about our sister-relationship, because all I feel just now is what's good about our habit of comfort and love, a habit that can only too quickly flip into something too familiar, exasperating even.

Like at Gloria's eighty-fourth birthday party, when Moss told us, "I love how *youtwo* rely on each other."

But Ev couldn't just say thank you and go on to something else. No, she had to analyze it, mess it up. "Now, if Libby learned to value me as I am," she said, "our sister-relationship would be even more wonderful. Some days Libby shuts me out with that weird humor of hers that cuts other people. You know how she gets with that. And other days she focuses too much on me."

I rolled my eyes at Gloria. The way Ev was talking about me made me think of those long-suffering couples you notice in restaurants who talk about each other only through others: waiters or friends or children.

"Libby was like that when she was three years old," Ev continued.

"Moss?" I said. "Would you please ask my sister if she figured all of that out when I was three and she was five?"

"Yes," Ev said, "I did. I just didn't have the proper terminology yet."

"Please." Times like this, I felt the two of us were rehashing all the games of growing up—the *I-dare-you* and the *I'll-tell* and the *you're-chicken*—games that drew us together and apart.

"Please what?" Ev probed.

"Please save me from your games. And from the proper terminology."

Gloria stretched herself. "I am a great masturbator," she pronounced.

Ev blinked.

I grinned at Gloria. "Good for you."

147

"It's a shame people don't talk about it openly."

Ev turned to Moss. "Would you please tell Libby that I did not invent what she calls the proper terminology."

"And tell Ev that she sure enjoys parading that terminology."

"Tell Libby that she enjoys being down on everyone, including me."

"Do not."

Moss sighed. She sounded content to be orchestrating our argument without having to say anything. Maybe to her this was just one other facet of our sister-relationship.

I leaned toward Moss. "Would you please ask my sister if she has ever considered that shutting her out, as she calls it, may have something to do with my schedule, now that she's only part-time at the shop? That I don't have much energy left?"

But Ev only shrugged. Her legal speed gave her unlimited energy, and she didn't understand that it wasn't like that for everyone. I could always tell when she was on speed: one, she talked more; and, two, whatever she began she finished quickly and thoroughly. Her homework. A quarrel. Cleaning. Repairs. All I had to do was steer her in the direction of what needed to be done most, hand her tools or a sponge, and watch her install coat hooks, say, or scrub the bathroom. Occasionally, speed made her charming, which was hard to watch, because charm was not really one of Ev's natural traits. She was too truthful for charm. Too solid-minded. But I didn't mention that speed changed her personality, because if I did she'd only get huffy with me, and then, if I'd get pissed, she'd try to win me back with charm. *You tell me.*

Gloria cut herself another piece of coconut cake. "Because it's a perfectly normal thing to do," she said.

I nodded. "I agree."

"Everyone does it."

"But no one talks about it," Gloria said. "About the different levels of skill involved. You have to practice before you become a great masturbator."

Tonight Ev's charm is just right for Basil as we sit on her robe above the river. She's admiring his fur, telling him what a beautiful shade of yellow it is. "The same color as the Cheney wheat fields, where we used to take you for long runs. Remember? Those roads that dipped into the sky? You always found the road again. Remember? Even when it seemed there was nothing but sky beyond the next hill."

I remind Basil how he chewed his way through a wall of Sheetrock when he was six months old. "When we came home, you and the floor were covered with white dust."

Stories.

Stories to keep death away from him.

Stories that are more for us than for him.

His ear twitches. He falls asleep. And I know how I will think back on this moment, replay it for myself—his ear twitching like this; his breath calm—and how incredibly alive he will have seemed to me. In this moment. Which already is passing. *Has passed.*

Once and again our hands touch as Ev and I continue to stroke him, as we whisper across him and ask one another if we're selfish, if we're tormenting him by keeping him alive. But who, then, are we, to choose death for anyone? With a human, we wouldn't consider that choice; yet, with an old, sick dog, that choice is pushed at us by our friends, by Dr. Sylvia, even by customers at the plant shop. Are we stalling for Basil's sake? For ours? Already, he feels lost to us. We tell each other that we're preparing to accept his loss, that we need time for that, and then we feel awful because, once again, we are talking about ourselves. Our suffering. Our grieving. It always comes back to that. And it's goddamn ugly.

"Let's swim." Ev stands up.

We let Basil sleep, climb down the steep path to the willows. As girls, Ev and I used to sit in the cradles of these willows, where the wide branches curve outward and up. I was six when my father taught me how to be safe in the river. Very few people swam in the Spokane back then, because it hadn't been cleaned up yet. Most houses were oriented away from the water, and their windows opened to the street. All that summer, every evening after closing the plant shop, my father would swim across the river with Ev and me. He prided himself on swimming in just about anything, but he was meticulous about showering afterward.

While my mother read seed catalogues and mystery novels—the only hour in the day that was hers alone—my father double-tied the straps of our orange life vests and taught us where to enter the current by estimating its speed. If it was fast, we'd plunge in upstream so that we'd end up directly across the river from our house, by the old cottonwood tree. We'd leap from the water like flying fish, hang on to the long branches, let the current tug at our legs. I'd strip off fistfuls of glossy cottonwood leaves—their tops a dark lime-green, their bottoms chalky green—and stuff them inside my swimsuit for my mother.

At home, I'd spread them on our picnic table for her, and

she'd bend across them, marveling how each leaf—not brittle and shriveled yet; not for another day—was held together by a net of raised veins. My mother understood about plants and had a reputation as a plant doctor. People wouldn't just come to our shop for new plants, but also to bring my mother their dwindling plants, their blotchy and spindly and infested plants, and she'd keep them until she'd nurtured them to health. It's what I do now that my parents live in Oregon. Some mornings when I arrive to unlock the shop, I discover a dying plant on the front steps—foundlings, my mother used to call those plants—and I take it in, check it over, administer to it the way my mother used to. Ev is good at taking care of the business side of the shop, but I have inherited my mother's gift, her intuition for plants. She told me so.

She also told me it wore down her spirit to live in this desert landscape that was parched by midsummer, to plant a garden each spring and struggle to keep it alive past July. That's why she and my father retired in Oregon, where the land has more rain than it needs. My mother loves the gray skies, the promise of rain. In her garden in Portland, rhododendrons grow like dandelions, their leaves always damp and shiny. The growing season starts at least a month earlier and lasts a month longer than in Spokane. Whenever we visit, I work with my mother in her lavish garden, while my father and Ev take hikes as they did when we were children. He believed in having quality walking shoes, just as he believed children should wear life vests till age twelve. It was a law he had grown up with, and he was not about to change it for his daughters. Even after Ev and I became confident swimmers, he still made us wear those bulky orange vests. I longed to be twelve, and I've never been as jealous as during those two years when Ev was allowed to swim without her vest and I still had to wear mine.

"Careful, now." My sister is pointing to the base of the willow, where the floods have cast off trash and rocks and fallen branches.

We have to scuttle around several heaps of the debris to get to the sandy recess where we skinny-dip some nights despite our awareness of the people who've drowned. With each day, it has become easier to overcome our reluctance to enter its current. "You must never let the dead spoil the river for you," my father taught us. And essentially we do feel safe. Because we've both studied the river since we were children. Learned not to misuse it. Not to ride it in borrowed boats or dive from bridges or tie ourselves to rafts. Acts like that invite the wrath of the river.

As we strip, light slips across my sister's gray hair, her narrow shoulders, her buttocks. It always astounds me how much brighter it is here on the water at night than just a short distance away in our garden. Gloria believes the river holds us within its own time zone, hours behind the rest of our neighborhood.

My sister glides into the water. "Libby?" she calls out, face raised to keep her heavy glasses dry.

Above us, on the hill, I feel Basil sleeping, and from the direction of Gloria's house comes the pulse of a drum—not a lesson, but Gloria drumming for herself. I always can tell the difference, because when she drums for herself, like this, her voice lives inside her drum, and I feel the tremor of her drumming—water and fire and earth—throughout my body, stretching my skin. But tonight Gloria is stretching me too wide. Stretching me wide open to sorrow—a season of sorrow—that fans out ahead of me like my sister's hair on the water. And suddenly I can't bear to follow Ev.

152

Lower Crossing

"Libby?" She is floating on her back, feet flickering. "Libby?"
I hug my bare breasts. Shiver.

My sister kicks shining ribbons of water toward me. "Aren't
you coming in?"

"I'm freezing," I tell her. It's easier than to explain how
water has forever been a place of bliss for me—for swimming
and diving and floating and that tonight I don't know how to
reclaim that bliss.

By mid-August, the river is no longer deep enough to ensnare
anyone, at least not in our neighborhood, where the water is
getting lazy. Low. Rocks that only a month earlier lay sub-
merged, are now crusted with gray and white like immense pre-
historic eggs.

Gloria and I wait for the day for our crossing. Late one afternoon, she calls me to the edge of my garden and motions to the
last wet boulders on the bottom of the riverbed. No white currents here—merely a flow so slight that it's impossible to deter-
mine in which direction it flows. Unless you know.

"Tomorrow morning," Gloria decides.

"Tomorrow morning."

But we don't have our crossing. Because right after I talk to
Gloria I can't find Basil. Ev and I walk around, knock on doors,
drive along both sides of the river, peer through the glass panel
of the barber's locked door. Nothing. We hunt for Basil along
the cliff where the old Shriners Hospital stands, long empty, its
cupola and stone wings a reminder of the children who stayed
within these walls.

By five in the morning, I have trouble staying awake. We're
driving through Manito Park, searching through the Perennial

Garden, the Rose Garden, and outside the fence of the Japanese Garden. When we circle the duck pond in the fading night, I open the window and turn on the silver flashlight I got at Eagle's last month.

"Another home improvement?" Ev teases me.

I yawn.

"We have more home improvements than we need, more than a convent—"

"Very good, Ev. Very catty."

"—more than a professional carpenter."

"Then I'll just buy something for Gloria next time. Some batteries for her vibrator."

"I can always tell when you're about to go for home improvements."

I swear my sister has a detector that tells her when I'm getting ready for sex. Except we call it home improvements. And in a way, it does improve our home life. Even afterward. Because our half-empty tube of caulking evokes Steve from Eagle's on Division, the glue gun Matthew from the South Hill Ernst's, the bicycle pump Hal from the General Store. *Home improvements.*

I shine my flashlight toward a huge ponderosa. "At least they're my age."

"Is that your only prerequisite?"

"You . . ."

"Yes?"

"Go on, have your intense study sessions with your young man."

"Between the two of us, we've really split up the entire mandepartment. Has that ever occurred to you, Libby?"

"I don't want to be analyzed. I'm so tired, I can barely hold this flashlight."

Ev stops the car.

"It's unlikely Basil made it this far anyhow. Uphill at that."

We get out. Lean against the side of the car.

Ev opens a prescription bottle, swallows two pills. "Let me give you some speed," she offers, and holds the bottle out to me.

I hesitate, such a good citizen when it comes to obeying the rule about not taking someone else's medication. "Sure," I say.

But when she hands me the bottle, it drops and the pills scatter on the ground. At least a dozen geese get to them before we can, jabbing, raising their heads as they swallow, the insides of their beaks voracious as they shriek for more.

"Jesus Christ," Ev says.

I rub my arms, wishing I'd worn my hooded sweatshirt instead of this cotton blouse. "What will they be like once the speed starts working?"

"Straight out of Hitchcock. The birds. Only worse. Dive-bomber geese."

"I don't want to be around for that."

"Well, they stole my speed. So they deserve it."

"That's vindictive." In the voice that Ev has used to analyze me, I add, "It is unprofessional to apply standards of human conscience and responsibility to animals."

She looks at me, sharply.

"It's not nice."

"Nice?"

"Not fucking nice. Okay? It's not fucking nice. Is that better?"

"I can't stand being near you when you get vulgar."

"Let's just find Basil." My voice skids. "Please?"

"Sure." She nods, eyes worried. Worried for me. "Sure, Libby."

Silently, we drive to our house, and after Ev parks her station wagon, we walk once again downstream along the river trail. A dank smell rises from the stagnant water. Dawn strips the parched embankment, reveals the barren earth. *A dangerous landscape to get lost in. For any living being.* Tumbleweeds careen across the cracked ground, yielding instant blooms of dust. What has survived of the vegetation here is amber and brown, as invariably this time of year.

When we pass a torn, matted blanket, I wonder if anyone slept on it last night. Basil maybe? "Basil?" I call his name, determined to make him safe once again.

Across the river, the hillside is still undeveloped. Scrawny bushes and trees straggle up the incline, where a structure of tarps and lumber hangs at a precarious tilt, half hidden by sumacs and weeds. Just a week ago this shack wasn't here. I'm terrified for the people who live in it. They feel endangered. Like Basil. How devastating it would be to look from a place like that across the water, to see the lamps in the houses of Lower Crossing, and to realize that the smoke rising from the chimneys means warmth for others—not you.

"You think I should drive around some more?" Ev asks. In her round face, her chin is skinny, so skinny. "You could check around here."

I stop. Touch her chin with one finger.

"Libby? What is it?"

"I want to know what happens when people . . . when they no longer have whatever it was that once used to . . . sustain them."

"Libby—"

"What happens then? When they no longer have that?"

"Maybe I should stay with you and look for Basil."

"No. It's better to search as many areas as possible. I'll double back close to the water."

She hesitates. With one shoe, she works free a pebble, nudges it toward a log.

"Go." I set my hands on her shoulders, gently, steer her in the opposite direction, and head toward the broken stone pillars that used to support a bridge. On the pebbled bank lies a rusted stovepipe, and I step across it and onto a flat rock that, until recently, was covered by water. Where the pillars jut from the riverbed, they obstruct the last trickle of current as it pursues its way around them.

It's getting lighter when I reach our neighborhood. Before starting up the hill to our house, I glance around once more. To the east, Monroe Street Bridge and the taller buildings of downtown. To the west—

Whimpering.

"Basil?" I ask softly. "Basil?"

And hear.

Whimpering. Again.

Hear him whimpering.

And start shouting: "Basil—oh my God—" I crash through tangled branches, crash toward the whimpering, and still I don't see him—not till I stop altogether and listen, listen hard—and there he lies, near the bottom of our path, where he must have been snagged all night, in one of those ditches carved by debris that the river dumped when it retreated

Basil tries to crawl toward me, whimpering, but his hindquarters are wedged beneath branches and briars.

"Don't . . ." I'm crying. "I'll get you out."

Still, he tries to hoist himself up again, launch himself in my direction as if he were forever the pup we took home from Spokanimal. But his legs tremble. Buckle.

Branches snap around me as I burrow toward his den, his prison. "I'll get you out."

He howls, barks, his throat raw, worn out overnight. While I didn't hear him. While I searched in the wrong places. While all along he was nearby.

"Sshhh," I murmur to him. "I'm almost there, Basil. Lie still. Ev and I looked for you all night. We did. We didn't sleep. Sshhh, Basil." What did he think all alone here? That this was the end? That he would never see us again? Twigs scratch my face, my arms, and I'm sweating hard. I want to have my hands on his long, sweet face, want to feel the life-warmth of his fur so much that I, too, tremble. Tremble with a love for him more fierce than anything I've felt for my sister or my parents. Because he is out of my reach now. So terribly close. And then—"*And then . . . ,*" *Jesse would say*—I'm crouching next to Basil, our feet in the shallow lick of river.

"Let's get you out of here, Basil."

I don't trust it, that river, suspect it of still plotting to claim my dog. But maybe being claimed by the river would be better for him than being deserted by his body. Carefully, I try to lift him across the barrier of twigs and trash and stones.

"*And then?*"

"*And then, Jesse, your grandmother will drum us a path right up this hill, and I'll carry Basil up to our house, and—*"

But it's not that easy. He's too heavy for me, and I have to set him back down. My belly feels tight. Queasy. "Stay," I tell Basil.

Lower Crossing

And laugh. "What else is there for you to do, huh?" With both hands and feet I thrash about, open a gap for us, all along continuing eye contact with Basil. "I promise I won't leave you behind. Ev gave me speed. I could shlep fifteen dogs like you up that hill. Fifteen hundred zillion dogs. You hear that?" I use my back to break us a wedge out of the thicket. "So don't you worry, Basil. I'll get you out of here. I will."

"And then, Libby?"

I raise Basil to his feet. But he is too shaky, too weak to stand alone. I straddle him without adding my burden to his, take off my blouse, and loop it beneath his belly. I hold on to the fabric, letting it support him so he doesn't have to carry his own weight. "We should get you some of Ev's speed. That's why I got tons of energy. Because of Ev's speed. I can do this for hours, Basil. For days. That's how strong I am. And with some of that speed, you'd be able to leap right out of here and up that hill."

But it takes us more than an hour to reach the top of the path that Basil used to race up in seconds—*bullet, my bullet*—coming at me grinning, tongue and tail flopping. "You were the fastest dog ever," I tell him. "Faster than Ev's divebomber geese on speed. How do you think they're feeling now, huh? Now, if Jesse were telling you about those geese, they'd be doing cartwheels in the sky. They'd swoop down for you, their wings one big parachute, and carry you up to the house."

Once I get him inside the house, Basil won't eat, won't even drink water. I drag his blanket from the kitchen into the living room, settle him in front of the fireplace, build him a summer fire to stop us both from shaking.

For five months Ev and I keep him going: with medicine; with food; with visits to Dr. Sylvia; with Basil stories that we've both heard before but need to hear again. Now and then we get silly with him, remind him how we chose him over his brother, even demonstrate how he liked to crouch low before doing his crazy dance around us. He blinks at my rendition of his crazy dance. Frowns, if it's possible for a dog to frown.

I remind him that we still have to hold our vigil outside the gay bar, take Ev along, and sit on the curb across from the bar. "You can sleep while we wait for the rednecks, but once they get there, you'll have to look ferocious."

When Gloria boils the hearts of five chickens for Basil, he refuses; but when she mashes them with fudge and potato chips—"Some bloody valentine," Ev sings—Basil scarfs the whole mess down the way he hasn't scarfed anything in months. So vigorously does he lick his bowl that it skids across the kitchen floor while he chases it with his tongue, lapping, jostling.

"Such a strong dog," Ev praises him.

"Protein plus the three major food groups," Gloria says. "Sugar, salt, and grease."

From then on we concoct Gloria's bloody valentine every day and grind Basil's medicine into it. We leave the house only for work or classes or groceries. No movies. No dinners out. We want to be home with Basil. For hours we sit with him by the fireplace, stroke his thick pelt, watch the river through the French doors, the trees as they cast off golden and red leaves in their own flowing motion. One morning we spot a bald eagle. The following day a moose swimming parallel to shore. We bring our father's binoculars from the attic, and whenever we

160

notice movement on the water, we report to Basil what's out there.

And it does slow our season of parting from him. Makes us easier with each other. One afternoon we count five deer in the clearing. From then on we count everything for him: geese, quails, song birds, squirrels. Friends bring food. Toys for Basil. A bird feeder. Our first bird at the feeder is plump and red-breasted. It arrives when Moss is visiting.

"A cardinal," Ev tells Basil. "Look at the cardinal. In the feeder out there. Basil? Look."

"I think cardinals have peaked heads," Moss says. "You really should learn the names before you confuse Basil."

Two days later she is back with a guide to Northwestern birds that she's bought at Auntie's Bookstore. We study the pictures, notice details we haven't seen that clearly before. As children we were always in motion, as adults too busy. Now we have made a choice to be here. To see. To take shifts with Basil.

He never recovers. That night by the river has hurled him forward into old age, has rendered him helpless. Once he is no longer able to raise himself to his legs, we rig up a canvas sling—our log carrier—to hold him up and help him outside. If he soils himself, he shifts his head aside as if to protect us from the shame in his eyes. Tenderly, we clean him up, tell him we don't mind. But away from him in the bathroom we gag, muffle the sounds so he won't hear us.

One Saturday afternoon Jesse tries to get Basil to raise his head by unwrapping the rawhide strips he's brought. Not too long ago, just the sound of cellophane would get Basil excited, but now he won't even sniff Jesse's hand when he extends the rawhide.

"He's hollow inside from hurting," Jesse explains. "And loopy."

"Loopy . . ." Ev says. "How do you mean loopy?"

"All loopy like with the moon at night and it being sunshine somewhere else but you can climb up behind the loopiness and climb up like a bear climbing a telephone pole like my dad when he went to the airport and then climbed up a telephone pole so he could get on the airplane and then I had to climb up the telephone pole when his airplane came back so I could get him back down."

"Now I understand exactly what it means," Ev says gently. "Thank you."

Early the following morning, before the Street Café opens, Moss comes over to give Basil one of her massages. She lies next to him on the rug, and while she kneads the toes on his front legs, she hums. It's become a ritual between them: she'll hum; he'll lean his snout against her high, curved forehead and close his eyes as if he were meditating with her. "There . . ." she'll say as she scoops her fingertips into the crevices between his black pads. "You like that, oh yes." And she'll progress to his hind legs, his flanks.

"Moss?" Ev asks. "Do you ever wish you had finished divinity school?"

"Not really." She keeps rubbing Basil's belly.

"You would have made a good minister."

"Yes. But I like this here better." She flattens her hands across Basil's ears. "It may be time . . . soon, to let Basilboy have his last nap?"

I nod. "It's what Dr. Sylvia says too."

But my sister is shaking her head.

Lower Crossing

"One more week?" I ask her.

"I can't—I can't do it, Libby."

"I'll go," Moss offers. "I'll go in your place, Ev."

"I hate to be like this. So selfish and—"

"It would freak Basilboy out to see you so upset," Moss says firmly. "Whoever goes with him has to stay calm."

"One more week," I tell Moss.

It's beginning to snow the morning Ev helps me to lift Basil onto the back seat of Moss's car. Ev has been saying goodbye to him for the last hour, and she's still stroking his head.

"Okay now?" I kiss her cheek, nudge her toward the house.

Then I slide in next to Basil, position him across my knees. For a large dog, he has become impossibly light. Jesse was right: all the hurting has indeed hollowed Basil out. Moss is backing up, jerking the stick shift as if she were Catherine the Great auditioning a horse. I feel awful: here I am with my dog on his way to die, and once again I'm thinking smut.

"I'm sorry, Moss," I say.

She glances at me in the mirror, doesn't ask what I'm sorry for, "It's okay."

As she drives north on Division, she hits a pothole, and Basil's head bounces against my breasts. He peers at me as if apologizing. Considerate even now. But most of all so very tired. There is no more puppy left in him.

I cradle him against me, whisper a lie. "It'll be all right . . . all right."

On both sides of Division, the stores and strip malls are still closed, making it seem that today hasn't begun yet, that we're on river time—*and why not?*—stuck in that time zone an hour or two behind everyone else, making us immune to whatever is to come. But as soon as I think that, it all changes, and we're driving fast, so fast—on fast-forward, that's how fast—until Moss brakes hard, swerves to the edge of the road.

I hold on to Basil. "Is it icy out there?"

Her tires crush tumbleweeds that are dusted with white, and as her car rocks to an abrupt halt, she's laughing. Laughing?

"Moss?"

"Talk about location." She motions to a billboard with an arrow: *Taxidermist. Turn Here.*

I stare at the billboard, at Moss, and then both of us are off laughing, a grim laughter that rides on tears.

"We could—" Moss hiccups. "We could bring Basilboy here."

He hears his name, raises his head weakly.

"Afterward," she adds. "Instead of letting them cremate him."

"And then what? Prop him up at the Street Café?"

"He'd look real handsome next to the cake display."

I'm howling with laughter. "You know how much that dog loves chocolate."

But when Moss turns to glance at Basil and me, it's plain that she isn't kidding.

"You're not kidding," I say.

"We can take him to the vet and then come back here with him."

"No, Moss." I slide one hand down my chin, wipe tears into my neck.

"I have two reasons. Okay?"

"Just two?"

"One: his fur is still full."

164

I run my hand up his back, make his thick yellow hair stand up, smooth it down again. At home, Ev will already have thrown out his fudge jar. Stored his toys and blanket in the attic. To shield me from anything that could possibly remind me of him. As if he didn't live inside my heart. From that, I don't need protection.

"And, two," Moss is saying, "he would look better stuffed than he did these last few months — not so skinny."

"No, Moss."

"The taxidermist can fix Basilboy up so he can stand by himself. And I'll pay half. You and Ev can split the other half."

"No, Moss."

"Or I can stuff him myself."

"You're not serious."

"I did taxidermy when I was fifteen. Because I loved the pizza man across from my high school."

"What does that have to do with—"

"He did taxidermy for a hobby."

"God, I hope he washed his hands."

"He had all those stuffed animals on pedestals along the walls of his pizza parlor. I asked if I could take lessons from him."

"Don't listen to her, Basil."

"I wanted to be around the pizza man more. Without gaining twenty pounds."

"Of course. How much pizza can anyone eat? The next logical step had to be taxidermy."

"His pizza wasn't that good. . . . But he taught me how to do a couple of birds. Small ones. A dove. Two parakeets. Then my brother's hamster died."

"Let me guess. You eternalized your brother's hamster."

"By then I was no longer interested in things that didn't breathe. I liked the expressions of the animals, their poses, but I wanted them in motion, and it was only natural that I stopped loving the pizza man. He never noticed—the love *or* the not-love. But I sent my brother to him. He still has the hamster. Except it's fatter now than it used to be."

"Sounds like your pizza man put too much stuffing inside."

"He was always putting too much cheese on pizzas."

For an instant there I think I hear the jiggling of Basil's collar, even though he's not moving, and I know I'll continue to hear that sound for months after he's dead. But now the jiggling is coming from Moss, from her knee against the key chain against the steering column as she starts the car and already we're in the vet's parking lot and I'm carrying Basil into Dr. Sylvia's office by myself—that's how light he is, how impossibly light—and Moss is steadying my arm while I stand next to a metal table, breathing animal fear and disinfectants, cradling Basil's head in my palms as I did once before when Dr. Sylvia was sticking a needle into him.

Except that day he did wake up again.

He was just a year old, and we'd been reluctant to get him neutered, because we didn't want to mess with his personality. Besides, we figured he'd outgrow his restlessness and stop barking by the door at dawn, ready to chase squirrels and skunks and pheasants and whatever else he might scare up in the undergrowth along the river.

Three evenings in a row he came home skunked so thoroughly that tomato juice wouldn't get the stink out of his fur. When Gloria said to rinse him with douche and water—a solution of one to four—I didn't want to, because I was embarrassed the cashier at Rosauer's might think I poured that kind of junk into myself when every self-respecting woman knows how bad it is for your insides. But Ev—simply to prove to me she didn't care what others thought of her—drove to Rosauer's and returned with a dozen bottles of douche in four flavors, just douche, not bothering to buy at least a few other items for camouflage. Then she bragged, of course, how she'd looked straight at the man who rang them up, daring him to make one single comment.

Turned out we needed just three bottles. That's how well the douche killed even the worst odors. Made me shudder to think what it's really sold for. Still, from then on we kept stocked up on douche, Ev's assignment.

One afternoon Basil ran home wailing, head fringed with porcupine quills that stuck out like Tammy Faye Bakker's eyelashes. Most of them we extricated, careful not to leave any ends in Basil's skin even though he thrashed about, his tongue swollen. We were afraid he was having convulsions, because he kept curling his tongue outward as if he were trying to push something from his throat. When Ev and I finally managed to pry his jaw apart, we could see that his gums and the roof of his mouth were pierced by dozens of quills, and we drove him to Dr. Sylvia's clinic.

To get rid of Tammy Faye, the vet said, she had to put Basil out. "You may as well get him fixed at the same time," she suggested. "It'll settle him down considerably. And it's the responsible thing to do."

Ev and I were too exhausted—from struggling with Basil; from dreading yet another skunking—to protest. "So he went in for porcupine quills and came out deballed," was the story we told our friends, "and he's been staying away from porcupines ever since."

It turned into the kind of story so familiar you hear yourself

using the same words, the same inflections, the same pauses—
all in the same sequence of words and inflections and pauses—
while already you anticipate the same laughter and even resort
to manipulating that laughter by starting it yourself. "So he
went in for porcupine quills and came out deballed . . ." *pause
pause pause*

Beneath my hands, Basil's skull feels gaunt—

pause pause " . . . and he's been staying away from porcupines ever since." *Laugh track. Turn it on. Blast it to its max.
Run it and rerun it.* "So he went in for porcupine quills and—"

"*And then?*" *Jesse asks me.*

Gaunt, so gaunt, his skull, beneath my hands—

"*And then?*"

Ah, Jesse. He's heard that old story many times, except for
him we substituted neutered for deballed. "So he went in for
porcupine quills and came out neutered . . ." *pause pause pause
laugh track number 15*

Dr. Sylvia sinks her needle into Basil—

*belly laughter louder laugh track number 17 laugh track
number* " . . . and he's been staying away from porcupines ever
since." Such a used-up story. And no longer funny.

"What does 'neutered' mean, Libby?" Jesse asked me the
first time he heard the porcupine story.

"So he can't make puppies."

"Why not?"

"Because— You have such good questions, Jess."

"Why not, Libby?"

"Because there are already too many dogs around that no
one takes care of."

"You and I can take care of Basil's puppies."

Lower Crossing

Dr. Sylvia's needle—

I try to evoke Basil as a puppy, but I can't see him. It's a failure of imagination. A failure of resurrection. All I get are fragments of him as a young dog: the hayloft smell of his fur, sun and dust; that slipped note when his barking turned high with excitement; the rumble of contentment in his belly after he ate. . . . But I cannot see him as a puppy.

That needle—

"—and he's been staying away from porcupines ever since."

Forever she sinks that needle into Basil, now—

"—been staying away from porcupines ever since staying away from porcupines ever since away from porcupines ever since from porcupines ever since porcupines ever—"

For what that needle is about to do, it is shockingly small. I want to look away from it, but I don't let myself. I hum to Basil, hum the way Moss does when she massages him. Moss knows. How to hum. How to stand close behind me—so quiet, quiet now—

"And then?" Jesse asks. "And then, Libby?"

Red frogs with three tongues. Drums made from the heads of lions and alligators. Home improvements. My mother in her rain-beaded garden. Eagles and moose. Moss's garbanzo stew. Bears that live in hedges. The green window in our plant shop. If I want to, I can believe what I already know in my gut: that what nurtures us, will also sustain us at times of pain if we choose to go there. *Geese doing cartwheels in the sky. The first apples on Gloria's trees. My father double-tying my orange life vest. Songbirds at our feeders. Stars talking to me through Jesse's glass roof. My sister and I walking to the edge of our garden. Far below us, the river flows heavy and gray and cold. But it doesn't have to be win-*

169

ter. It can be summer. Still and again. And my sister can enter the current. I can follow her, immerse myself in whatever pain and loss are mine, let myself sink beneath the surface, where the river will continue to carry me. Whenever I emerge to tears, I search for my sister's shining back and follow once again until she reaches the opposite bank, and when she grips a branch of the cotton-wood tree, I'll leap for one close to hers. While the current guides our legs downstream, my sister and I hold on to the supple branches, arms taut, while the rest of our bodies are floating. Floating that feels like flying.

I trace the familiar ridge of bone up the length of Basil's head between his eyes and ears—so quiet, quiet now—and take my hands from him, release him. And still feel the imprint of his skull. When I flatten my palms against each other, preserving Basil between them, I finally can see him, a yellow pup, tongue flopping—*bullet, my bullet*—running toward me at dusk. I can go there again—to that place at dusk where Basil runs toward me forever. Where Basil swims with Jesse, though he never liked the water. *Floating that feels like flying, Jesse. Flying that feels like floating. While all along the river continues to hold the light. Holds us the way it holds the light. The way I hold on to the cottonwood branches. I reach up with one arm. Seize a handful of leaves. A few of them will get away when we swim home, but the rest I'll stick into a vase. Come morning, they'll still have the texture of heavy silk.*

About the Author

Ursula Hegi is the author of eight critically acclaimed books, including *Intrusions, Floating in My Mother's Palm, Stones from the River, Tearing the Silence,* and *The Vision of Emma Blau.* She lives in New York State.